THE TRUTH IN NIGHTMARES

The candle flamed higher, and a tiny stream of dark red wax began to spurt down its sides, splashing an uneven red pattern on the wooden floor. Agatha's eyes were wider now, filling with terror. A department store mannequin flashed through her mind. It was pouring blood. A fiery sword flashed through the air. Her world was red. She was remembering a very brutal, violent dream she had experienced several weeks before . . . Only it wasn't a dream . . . She had heard it all. The violence . . . The murder . . . *She had been awake the night he was killed. She had heard the whole thing* . . .

Other Avon Books by
Thomas Hauser

MISSING

Coming Soon

THE TRIAL OF PATROLMAN THOMAS SHEA

AGATHA'S FRIENDS

THOMAS HAUSER

AVON
PUBLISHERS OF BARD, CAMELOT, DISCUS AND FLARE BOOKS

AGATHA'S FRIENDS is an original publication of Avon Books. This work has never before appeared in book form.

AVON BOOKS
A division of
The Hearst Corporation
959 Eighth Avenue
New York, New York 10019

Published by arrangement with the author
Library of Congress Catalog Card Number: 82-90518
ISBN: 0-380-82222-9

First Avon Printing, February, 1983

Printed in the U. S. A.

WFH 10 9 8 7 6 5 4 3 2 1

Despite the incidental use of actual names and places, the characters and incidents portrayed in this book are wholly fictional.

For my brother, Jim

AGATHA'S FRIENDS

There was a rat in her bed. Aggy knew it. Trembling, she closed her eyes tight, sealing off the world outside.

"Wake up!" something told her. "Wake up!"

A furry body brushed against her.

She screamed.

Tiny claws clutched at her side.

Again, she screamed, and hurled herself out of bed onto the floor.

What . . . Where . . .

It was five o'clock in the morning.

Heart pounding, she pulled back the covers.

Nothing . . . Always nothing . . .

Someday, she'd fucking explode. And when she did, Rubes and Matt, wherever they were, would be splattered to pieces. That was a promise.

CHAPTER 1

Matthew Paul Reuben, misnamed if one considered the attributes of the apostles, whistled as he walked. Autumn was his favorite time of year. Summer in New York City was too hot, winter icy cold, and spring too short. That left autumn, which was acceptable. Especially the hours before noon, when Matt could walk the winding path by the lake in Central Park without rubbing shoulders with the assorted beings who ran rampant in Manhattan every Saturday and Sunday afternoon.

At ten o'clock on Sunday morning, the park was free of refuse. A few people were walking dogs; an occasional jogger wheezed by in masochistic ecstasy. Mostly though, Matt was alone, without the steel bands, roller skaters and beat of conga drums that dominated the park in later hours. He liked it that way. His cheerful tune angled off the trees, and the crunch of leaves—red, brown, gold—beat a crisp accompaniment beneath his feet.

As the morning sun emerged from behind the confines of a solitary cloud, Matt pulled at the snaps of his brown suede jacket, and the garment opened loosely over his twenty-nine-year-old frame. Not muscular but well built, on the slender side with shoulders much broader than appeared at first glance. As the result of endless parental pressure, his posture was erect. Not rigid, but he never lost an inch of his six feet plus to slouching. His smile—warm with little-boy appeal—was the key to his good looks. There was something about his eyes a person might not trust. A woman he had gone out with once said they typified a guy who would walk through a revolving door and let the people in front and behind do the pushing. But the smile was a good one. It blended well with his features and rarely failed him. Matt had learned to turn it on and off at will and, if anyone said they didn't like it, that was sour grapes.

Twenty yards down the path, two girls in their mid-teens walked toward him. Timing the gesture with precision, Matt waited until they were within a few feet, then looked directly into the eyes of the taller of the two. The girl, clad in blue jeans, long dirty blonde hair reaching to her shoulders, blushed. Her companion giggled. His spirits lifted slightly by the confrontation, Matt walked on.

The path turned left and he followed. Walking west across the park, this was his usual route. Coming home, he'd pass to the north by Belvedere Castle and the reservoir. Walking, Matt told himself, was a greatly underestimated mode of transportation. It was cheap, good exercise and rather enjoyable. It made the most mundane of tasks rest lighter. He shook his head. Going to see Rubes wasn't all that bad. If he went for brunch, he could leave when he wanted. Get there at eleven; eat, talk for a half hour, then run.

Matt thought of his younger brother with an assurance that came from having been first out of the womb by several years. Sometimes the realization that he had been on top and Rubes on the bottom forever made him a bit uncomfortable. Better that way though, than the other way around. And besides, Rubes was resigned to his position. The competition, if there had ever been one, was over and, by acclamation, Matt had won. He was the rising account executive. Rubes taught sixth-grade math. Matt had his pick of women. Rubes sort of took what was left over.

"It's no big thing," Rubes told his older brother in what had amounted to a concession speech several years earlier. "I've finally realized I don't have to copy everything you do. After all, it's okay for a person to be himself."

Still, to ease whatever feelings of guilt he might have, once a month Matt went to Rubes's apartment for brunch, where they shared one of those awful gooey omelets that Rubes took such pride in making. The journey fulfilled an obligation. And, outside of Rubes, there wasn't much family left. Mother was involved with her own affairs and had made it clear that interference would not be tolerated. Father had died of a heart attack nine years ago.

The path turned again and led Matt past an ornate fountain at the park's core. A sizable crowd—mostly Latin, mostly young—had already begun to gather. Broad patches of brown scarred the once-green terrain. Near the fountain, salsa music was being played. Matt walked on, emerging from the park on 72nd Street and making his way west against the flow of pedestrian traffic. Past Broadway, the crowd thinned. He walked for another block and, shielding his eyes against the sun, turned up West End Avenue. Two blocks ahead, sitting on a concrete stoop, his brother waited. As Matt approached, Rubes looked up from the newspaper in front of him and jumped to his feet. His hair, no longer than Matt's, was perpetually in need of combing. As he rose, it flopped down in the direction of a warm, slightly goofy smile.

"Matt, hi! Hey, your hair's getting longer. It looks great."

"Yeah, I add a little to it every day."

"No, really. It looks good. How was the walk over?"

"Okay."

There was an awkward moment.

"It's good to see you," Rubes said at last. "Listen, come on upstairs. I have all the stuff for an omelet."

Rubes led and Matt followed. His brother's apartment, Matt was fond of saying, was "the norm for the West Side"—a high-ceilinged living room dotted with secondhand furniture and a small bedroom barely large enough for the mandatory double bed. A tiny kitchen alcove, which comfortably stood two and seated no one, was off to the side.

Settling in a worn overstuffed chair near the door, Matt reached for the sports section of the paper, but Rubes interrupted.

"Come on in the kitchen and keep me company while I cook."

"Okay; it's your morning."

Rubes laughed. "Remember how Mom used to say that, on birthdays or something special when we'd spend the day together? 'Okay, it's your day; it's your morning.' "

"Yeah, I remember." Matt lifted himself from the chair and moved to the kitchen. For reasons he never understood, Rubes always insisted on harking back to the past as though it had been a great time or something.

Rubes took a quart of orange juice from the refrigerator and set it down on a table overlooking the street.

"Dating anyone in particular?" Matt asked.

The question, Rubes knew, was a prelude to a recitation of Matt's latest conquests.

"Yes."

Matt's face registered surprise. "No kidding. What's her name?"

"Aggy."

Matt made a face.

"Actually, it's short for Agatha. She works in a day-care center. I mentioned her to you a few weeks ago. We met in college and went out two or three times, but she wasn't that interested back then. I saw her by chance on the street a couple of months ago, and things picked up again."

"Where does she live?"

Rubes crossed back to the kitchen and began cracking eggs into a medium-sized glass bowl. "Two blocks up the street, in a brownstone at 366 West End Avenue."

Matt forced a smile. "That's right. Now I remember. She's the one who's geographically desirable."

"We're going to the park this afternoon. I told her I'd pick her up after brunch. Do you want to come?"

"I can't. I'd like to, but I have a date."

Matt always had a date. It was another of life's inequities that Rubes had spent the better part of his twenty-five years in pursuit of that elusive commodity known as a girlfriend, while Matt was always screwing some girl who looked like Farrah Fawcett, Bo Derek or whoever else happened to be in style. Outside of the high school Senior Prom, which Matt and his mother had made him go to, Rubes hadn't had a date until he got to college. Not that he was exactly a house on fire then. One date in September of his freshman year, none in October, one in November. In December, he met Lori. She was average-looking, with sagging breasts and a flabby rear end. She had made it with three guys in her first four months on campus and was beginning to feel experienced. She had no idea what to do in bed and Rubes, being a virgin, knew less. He went out with her three times and slept with her once.

Aggy though, was something special. Rubes met her in his junior year at Columbia, right after a monster snowstorm that had all but shut the city down. By then, he had forsaken Friday-night mixers and begun to prowl the university library system as his main source of women. By picking up his books and moving from reading room to reading room every two hours, Rubes could cover the entire Columbia-Barnard library system in three nights—no mean achievement if he did say so himself. With considerable awkwardness which it pained him to remember, one evening he had managed to pick up Aggy. Since then, he had come to suspect that it was the other way around. That didn't make sense though, since Aggy was close to beautiful and he was rather ordinary-looking.

Aggy had long straight black hair, a pretty face, great legs and a nice body. She was warm, she was bright, and Rubes liked her more than he had ever liked anyone before. It lasted three dates. Then, one afternoon after class, she told him she didn't want to see him anymore. Bingo! There it was again—endless suffering.

Rubes still remembered sitting in his apartment that night waiting for the tears to dry. Aimlessly, he turned on the television to watch a show about lawyers. At nine-thirty, he watched a western. At the first advertisement, he got up and made himself a milk shake. Just before ten, he went to the kitchen, took a miniature frozen pizza out of the refrigerator and put it in the oven. At the next ad, he put it on a plate and cut it into eight small pieces. He finished the last piece just before the eleven o'clock news, then went to bed as an escape mechanism. "Why can't I be happy?" he asked himself. "Is that asking so much? That's all I want. That's what everyone wants. Why can't I be happy?"

And now, years later, Rubes's world was coming together. At age twenty-five, after a lifetime of crap, he had a job he liked, a world he could live in and, most of all, by virtue of a chance reunion, he had Aggy.

For as long as Rubes could remember, he had lay in bed at night and fantasized about the woman who wasn't there. How, someday, he would fall in love and she would love him. How he'd lean over in bed and kiss her and tell her how much he cared. And now, maybe, just maybe, it was on the verge of becoming a reality.

"Matt, you have to meet her. How about this afternoon?"

"I really can't today. But soon, Rubes, very soon. I promise."

CHAPTER 2

As was usually the case when he came for brunch, by one o'clock Matt was gone. Rubes walked him to the door, watched him disappear downstairs, and closed the door behind him. Then, turning on the radio, he fiddled with the dial until he found the Jets football game and began stacking dishes in the sink. He was compulsively neat about some things and maddeningly sloppy about others. Dirty dishes fell into the first category. About the same time the Jets lost a fumble in their own end zone, Rubes ran the last of the soapy water down the drain and wiped the counter clean with a worn sponge. Then he flipped off the radio, stuffed his wallet and keys in a back pocket, and pulled a denim jacket from the closet.

"The camera," he reminded himself. "Don't forget the camera."

Outside, the blue sky and midday sun lent an uncharacteristically fresh air to Manhattan. At street level, Rubes took several unhurried breaths and began walking north. He liked West End Avenue. It was one of the few streets in Manhattan zoned against commercial traffic, which made it cleaner and less noisy than most of the city. Half a block from the concrete stoop that marked the front of Aggy's building, he debated briefly whether to go upstairs or buzz the intercom and wait outside. Opting for chivalry, he buzzed once and pushed open the seldom-locked front door. Aggy was waiting in the doorway when he reached the third-floor landing.

Rubes kissed her hello and stepped inside. The apartment was a large L-shaped studio filled with plants. Two broad beams divided the ceiling into three sections. A stone fireplace covered with multicolored begonias split the far wall. A spindly five-foot avocado stood off to the side. Three pots filled with Swedish ivy hung by a large bay window overlooking the street.

"I'll be with you in a minute," Aggy said. "I have to put my socks on."

Rubes made a face.

"No complaints," she warned.

The socks had been a point of mock controversy since the night two months earlier when Rubes and Aggy were on the verge of making love for the first time. Aggy was on her bed, naked from the waist up, and Rubes's mind was something of a blur since (1) they were stoned; (2) every time he looked at Aggy's long black hair and perfect smile, he got slightly dizzy anyway; and (3) he was very nervous and hoped he wouldn't be impotent. That was when Aggy took off her jeans and revealed a pair of red and white horizontally striped socks stretching to her knees.

Stunned silence.

"What's the matter? Don't you like my legs?"

"Your legs are fine. The socks look like something out of *The Wizard of Oz.*"

"Love me, love my socks. We're not severable."

Rubes took the package. In time, he even came to accept the socks, although he was still glad Aggy's jeans covered them up in public.

As Aggy rummaged through a bureau drawer, Rubes cast his eyes around. The apartment had a schizophrenic look. One wall—"my hero wall," Aggy called it—was covered with photos torn from newspapers and magazines—George McGovern, Willie Nelson, Bjorn Borg, Roberta Flack . . . Next to them, hanging from a strand of framing wire, a Confederate Army cavalry cutlass angled down. Tarnished by the neglect of generations, its long curved blade pointed toward books that ranged from Jean-Paul Sartre to Judith Krantz. A pile of papers on the desk nearby was topped by a flyer for a course in "Witchcraft, Magic and Sorcery" being given at the American Museum of Natural History. A needlepoint pillow lay on the floor.

"Here they are," Aggy announced triumphantly, taking a pair of blue socks with large orange triangles from the bureau and pulling them up under her jeans. Once they were secure, she straightened her pants legs and slipped on a pair of shoes. She looked good.

On the surface at least, Agatha Tilden was one of those people for whom everything went right. Twenty-five years old, brown eyes, teeth that sparkled. Her features seemed chiseled out of marble and then, somehow, colored and softened to provide a warm, gentle look. Her body, Rubes knew, was better than anyone had a right to expect, although she tended to wear clothes that deemphasized her curves. She had never dated anyone who hadn't asked her out a second time. It was Aggy, not men, who ended her relationships, and she took that for granted. Over the years, she had been dumped only once—a few months ago—actually, not so much dumped as abandoned. The guy had been good-looking, about thirty. They had met casually, and later he called to invite her for dinner. They'd gone out together a half dozen times when she learned she was pregnant.

There was never really any doubt in Aggy's mind that she would have the abortion. Except it wasn't all that easy. She hadn't realized how scary it would be; how it would dominate her thoughts, her dreams, and the course of her everyday life. There were a lot of emotional hassles, and she needed support. The guy hadn't provided any.

"I'm going to the clinic Thursday afternoon. Will you come with me?"

"I can't," he told her. "I have an appointment."

"Can't you change it?"

"No . . . Look, I know you're upset, but it will be over in a few days."

"Don't you realize what's happening inside of me? That's my baby." She turned from her own words, knowing how ugly they sounded to him.

"I don't want it," he said. And then his tone softened, not so much out of compassion as from fear that she just might talk herself into having the baby, and he didn't want some kid that was half his sperm running around.

"Look, I know you're upset," he said again. "But it's the only thing to do. It's not fair for you to be tied down for years because of an accident."

Then he offered to pay for the whole abortion instead of half. Aggy said half was all she wanted. He gave her cash.

The next few nights, Aggy hadn't slept very well. The final evening, she sat in a rocking chair by the window and read until midnight. Then she put the book down and rocked herself and her baby to sleep. She wasn't religious; she didn't believe in God. But, that night, she wanted something to hold onto. If there was a heaven, she told herself, the child would be better off in it. The following morning, she had the abortion.

The guy called that night to see how she was doing. Actually, he called to make sure she had done it.

For three days, Aggy stayed inside the apartment. A counselor at the abortion clinic had given her the name of a psychiatrist to call in case she became uncontrollably depressed, but she had always taken care of herself and wasn't about to give in to what she regarded as self-indulgence. Then, Saturday night, she realized there wasn't any food in the refrigerator and she hadn't eaten much of anything lately. With considerable effort, she put on some clothes, combed her hair, and tramped downstairs to face the world, or as much of it as would be encountered on the way to the delicatessen.

The trip took her five years into the past. On the corner of West End Avenue and 72nd Street, all alone at ten-fifteen on a Saturday night with the *New York Times* tucked under his arm, she'd seen Rubes. And Rubes had listened sympathetically while she told him all.

* * *

"Central Park or Riverside?" Rubes asked after Aggy had finished dressing and they'd reached the street.

"Riverside; it's less crowded, plus it's closer and I'm tired. I didn't sleep well last night."

"How come?"

"I don't know. Bad dreams, I guess."

Reaching out, Rubes slipped his arm around her waist. A little uncomfortable, Aggy let it stay without responding in kind. Rubes had his good points, but she found it hard to get excited about them. Lately, they'd been sleeping together on their once-a-week date, but not making love. He was so passive; sometimes she wished he'd scream or do something, anything, that registered emotion.

"There's an extra plus to Riverside," he said cheerfully. "It runs by the West Side Highway. If you close your eyes, the cars whizzing by sound like the roar of the ocean."

"Great! Now if I go to Cape Cod, every wave will sound like cars whizzing by on the West Side Highway." Suddenly, she pulled loose and pointed at the camera in his free hand. "What's that?"

"A camera."

"I know it's a camera. What's it for?"

"Taking pictures of you."

"No way!" she said.

Momentarily flustered, Rubes tugged at his sleeve. "Why not?"

"I don't want you to take my picture. That's all."

"But I've wanted to for a couple of weeks."

"Too bad. I have no desire to wind up in a box in someone's closet. Besides, you'd be much better off taking pictures of a flower. They're very photogenic, and flowers always smile."

Tentatively, he reached for her hand, then thought better of it and let his own dangle. "You're being silly."

"That's my prerogative."

"And you've been awfully jumpy lately."

"Look! We're going for a walk, not a picture-taking session. And, if it's all the same, I'd appreciate your laying off the heavy-duty psychoanalysis. In fact, why don't we both shut up."

"Huh?"

"You heard me. I'd like to walk without talking, just for a moment. It's no big crime on a sunny day to let your mind wander."

Rubes shrugged. "Okay! Whatever you want."

Her mother and father had slept in twin beds with a highly polished mahogany night table between them. It could have been a moat with crocodiles. Aggy's mother wore her hair long. When Aggy was little, she bit her fingernails and, because her father told her not to, she'd chew at the skin around her cuticles until the fingers reddened and filled with pus.

Pieces dislodged from an ill-fitting past. Maybe they'd never fit.

CHAPTER 3

Lieutenant Richard Marritt of the New York City Police Department was pissed. After seventeen years on the force, the last eight as a plainclothes detective, he was on patrol-car duty with a twenty-two-year-old rookie named Jim Dema on a six-hour shift for which neither man would be paid.

The cops in New York always got shafted. Consolidated Edison never gave the city free electric power. The banks never lowered the interest rate on municipal bonds. The cops? Thanks to the city's perpetual fiscal crisis, they were all working an extra twenty hours for free so the bankers and Con Ed executives wouldn't get mugged on the way home. And, to add insult to injury, the precinct captain had asked if Marritt would "mind" spending ten of those twenty hours on routine patrol.

The police dispatcher's voice came over the patrol-car radio at 3:35 P.M.: "There's a request that someone check out a third-floor apartment at 366 West End Avenue. Are any of you cars in the vicinity?"

The rookie turned toward Marritt, who shook his head in the negative. Quitting time was four o'clock, and the detective planned on getting back to the precinct house ten minutes early so he could leave the minute his shift was up.

"Second call," intoned the dispatcher. "Speak up out there in radio-land."

"What do you want checked?" Dema asked into the two-way radio set in the dashboard in front of him.

"The superintendent says something stinks in an apartment on the third floor. He tried his passkey, but it didn't work. Either the tenant changed locks or the lock is jammed."

"Who lives there?"

Marritt glared at the rookie, who seemed not to notice.

"Some guy about twenty-nine or thirty named Doug Nicholas. The super says he hasn't seen him for a couple of weeks."

Dema swerved left to avoid a pothole and turned the patrol car down West End Avenue. "We'll take it."

"Christ," Marritt muttered. "Something stinks and everyone gets excited. Probably, someone went on vacation and left a roll of rotten bologna on the kitchen table; or smelly cheese maybe."

Dema pulled the car to a halt in front of 366 West End Avenue, and Marritt got out on the right-hand side. "Stay here," he instructed the rookie. "It'll be quicker if I go alone."

The superintendent was waiting just inside the front door. Marritt recognized him as the middle-aged Italian who brought a bottle of whiskey to the station-house every Christmas Eve, and the cop's annoyance subsided slightly. The old man took care of six or seven buildings in the neighborhood and worked his butt off. Still, as the super led the way upstairs, Marritt realized for the thousandth time that he didn't like going into brownstones. There was never a doorman and the halls were usually dark and dingy. A cop never knew who or what waited inside. Also, brownstones didn't have elevators and, after seventeen years on the force, Marritt wasn't in the same shape he had started out in. At the third-floor landing, he was breathing heavily.

"That one, there," said the superintendent, pointing to the heavy wooden door on the courtyard side of the corridor.

The cop walked to the door and tried turning the handle. The automatic lock held firm. "Do you have a passkey?"

"It doesn't work."

"I didn't ask if it worked. I asked if you had one."

The superintendent reached into his pocket and thrust the key forward.

"Jesus, that's a pisser," Marritt said.

"What is?"

"That smell." Waving the old man back, Marritt drew his pistol and fired two shots into the lock. Tiny metal slivers showered the floor. Then, turning the handle to the left, he lowered his shoulder and pushed hard against the door. The shattered lock gave way and the door swung open.

The human body, Marritt had learned at the police academy, is biodegradable—to wit, when it stops functioning, it decomposes. But neither the academy nor all his years on the force had prepared him for this. Stretched out on the floor in front of him was a grisly composition of flesh, dried blood and bone, wrapped in a blood-caked shirt and jeans. The victim's hair had begun to come loose, and the face was a road map for maggots. Two stumps that had once been arms protruded from the bloated body. The skin was wet and blackish-blue. Rivers of blood lay clotted on the hardwood floor. The assault on his senses drove Marritt back against the wall. His knees wobbled and he gasped for air. The room reeked of death.

A menacing hiss punctured the heavy air. Marritt

turned. A large gray cat with blood on its whiskers and paws, a blue satin ribbon tied loosely around its neck, advanced slowly from the corner. Stopping at the corpse, like a jungle animal it began to feed. The detective drew his pistol and fired into the wall. The cat's head remained buried in its prey. The cop fired a second time, and the animal's skull exploded.

The homicide squad arrived a half hour later. Two paramedics cut the clothes off what was left of the body while a third cop set down chalk marks. Marritt, his composure regained, fired questions and orders in rapid sequence. "Can you tell what killed him?" he asked the senior paramedic.

"Five to ten stab wounds in the back and side. Two in the neck. It's hard to tell exactly how many."

"Anything in his pockets?"

"No, sir."

"Throw the clothes in the body bag. They're swarming with bugs."

The paramedics did as ordered.

"Get the body out of here."

The two paramedics put the corpse in the bag, leaving behind the white chalk outline of a human form. Only then did Marritt think to open a window. Then, turning to Dema who had come upstairs to survey the scene, he resumed his questioning.

"Is the knife still here?"

"No, sir."

"Shit."

"There's a puddle of dried wax on the bureau," the young cop offered. "It looks like a pretty big candle that burned down and overflowed its saucer. My guess is that he was killed at night."

"Maybe," the detective answered.

"His wallet and watch are still on the desk," the

younger man added. "It doesn't look like robbery was the motive."

Marritt glanced at the unmade bed, then at the floor, which was littered with magazines, socks, plates and the moldering remains of what had once been an apple. Three large posters advertising a concert by the rock group Kiss were on the far wall. "With all those stab wounds," he said at last, "it could have been a crime of passion."

Dema fell silent.

"We don't have much to start with," the detective went on, "so we'll go from scratch. I want fingerprints from the bureau and desk drawers. Forget about the doorknob. My sweaty palm took care of that. Run a print check on the inside door panel. Then we'll search the place." Marritt turned to the superintendent. The old man had not spoken since the cop shot the lock off the door. "Did you know any of his friends?"

The old man shook his head.

"I'll want to talk with everyone in the building, starting with whoever lives across the hall. This was a pretty messy murder. If it happened at night, someone must have heard it."

The apartment still stank. Shaking his head, Marritt walked out into the corridor and peered at the nameplate on the nearest door:

3B
Agatha Tilden

CHAPTER 4

Richard Marritt sat on the couch opposite the spindly avocado and spread his hands across his knees. Dema, note pad in hand, stood off to the side. Aggy and Rubes, just back from the park and not yet comfortable with the covey of police in her apartment, sat silent on the floor, looking first at the detective in his creased sixty-dollar suit and then at the younger uniformed cop.

They were an odd couple, Aggy thought. Marritt was heavyset, in his early forties, with black hair and an old-movie tough-guy look. Dema was twenty years younger, lean and fair-skinned, with light brown hair. For a moment, she focused on the rookie but, when their eyes met, he averted his gaze. "Maybe he doesn't like women," she told herself. That was okay. There were times she didn't like men very much either.

Marritt, meanwhile, was mulling over the day's events and giving Rubes a slightly sour look. The detective would have preferred to talk to the girl alone. Boyfriends were a nuisance. He had never met one who didn't feel the need to be helpful—to wit, answer questions that weren't meant for him—and overprotective—i.e., do all the talking. The end result was inevitably that Marritt didn't get answers from the person he wanted to talk with. Rubes's presence was a clear minus, but there wasn't much that could be done about it.

"Outside of the fact that he's dead," Marritt began, "we don't know much about Doug Nicholas. We know he was stabbed close to a dozen times, and we think it happened about three weeks ago at night. We don't have the murder weapon, and the preliminary report is that whoever killed him didn't leave any fingerprints. We've got an address book and a few other bits of information from the apartment but not much. I'd appreciate anything you can tell us."

"What do you want to know?" Aggy asked.

"Eventually, everything, but let's start with a few basics. Do you have any idea who might have killed him or why?"

Aggy shook her head.

Marritt was visibly annoyed. "You didn't think about the question." He leaned forward, and the couch wobbled slightly under his weight. "I know this is upsetting, and I can tell you from experience that it will get worse before it gets better. It hasn't sunk in yet that the person who lived across the hall has been murdered and, when it does, you won't sleep well for a couple of nights. But I need your help, and I want you to dig into your mind for anything that can help us. Did you know any of his friends?"

Again, Aggy shook her head. "Doug was usually alone. I mean, he was always friendly to me, but I never saw him with the same person more than once or twice."

"What about girls? Was he close to anyone?"

"Not that I know of."

"When did you first meet him?"

"I moved in about two years ago. Doug was already here."

"Did he have many visitors?"

"Yes."

"Would you care to elaborate?"

Marritt waited, but there was no response. Instead, Aggy stared off into space.

"Miss Tilden, could you tell me a little more about the visitors you just mentioned?"

"I'm sorry. What did you say?"

"I asked, could you tell me about Doug Nicholas's visitors?"

"Doug was a dealer. He sold drugs."

Marritt's eyebrows lifted.

"Not heroin or anything like that," she added. "A lot of grass, hash—the sort of stuff that's pretty much accepted."

"Did he have a job?"

"I guess not. He hung around a lot during the day; went to museums, read books. I suppose dealing was his business."

"How do you know he was a dealer?"

The hesitation in answering was longer.

"Don't worry," the cop assured her. "This won't get you in trouble."

"We were neighbors. We lived across the hall from one another. You pick up on that sort of stuff."

"Did you buy from him?"

Another pause.

"Once or twice, I bought an ounce."

"How friendly were you with each other?"

"I didn't like him very much."

"Why not?"

"He wasn't my type."

Aggy was starting to tighten up, and Marritt shifted his line of questioning. "What about the visitors you mentioned? How often did they come?"

"A couple of times a day, I guess. People would come, and Doug would buzz them in on the intercom. They'd come upstairs, stay for a few minutes, and leave."

"What were they like?"

"I don't know . . . nondescript. They never caused any trouble. They usually came at a decent hour. I suppose they bought what they wanted and left."

"After paying for it?" Marritt prodded.

"I guess so."

"How much money—" Marritt broke off in mid-sentence. "You started to say something else."

"It wasn't much," she said. "Once, I remember, someone came and buzzed about three in the morning. Doug was annoyed. He must have been afraid the neighbors would complain if people came to see him at odd hours of the night."

"Do you remember when that was?"

"I really don't."

"Do you generally keep your door closed?"

"Yes."

"How do you know he had visitors?"

"I'd hear them through the wall. His apartment is across the hall, but the stairs lead past my door and his buzzer is hooked up to the same circuit as mine. When I'm home, I hear it."

Marritt returned to the predawn visitor. "Do you have any idea who it was who came that time late at night?"

Again, Aggy was staring off into space.

"Miss Tilden."

"Huh?"

"I asked you a question."

"I'm sorry."

A department-store mannequin flashed through Aggy's mind.

"Miss Tilden, do you have any idea who it was who came that time late at night?"

"No."

"Did it happen more than once?"

"Not that I know of."

"Do you remember hearing anything that evening that might be helpful?"

"No."

"I want you to concentrate. Are you sure you can't remember anything?"

Aggy strained. "Nothing."

"What did they say? They must have said something for you to know that Doug was annoyed."

Again, the mannequin.

"All I remember is the buzzer, and someone coming upstairs. Then Doug said, 'You know better than to come here at three o'clock in the morning.' That's it," she said triumphantly. "It was three in the morning. He said, 'You know better than to come here at three o'clock in the morning. You'll wake the whole building.'" Her euphoria subsided. "That's all I remember. I don't know who or when it was."

"Did you hear a name?"

"No."

"Are you positive?"

"Yes."

"Did the other person say anything?"

"Not that I remember."

Marritt had followed the avenue as far as it would lead. Again, he shifted subjects.

"Do you know how much money Doug kept in the apartment?"

For the first time, Rubes interrupted. "Have you searched it?"

"None of your fucking business," Marritt thought to himself . . . "Yes," he answered placidly. "We didn't find anything." Marritt turned his attention back to Aggy. "Do you know what he kept around the apartment . . . money or drugs?"

Aggy furrowed her brow, more from edginess than thought. "Once a month, Doug would be gone for a few days. I think he'd fly to someplace in Texas, bring back a shipment, and sell it in small amounts."

"Do you have any idea where he kept his cache?"

She was pushing her mind now. "Maybe. One afternoon, I went over tc Doug's apartment just to chat. He hadn't been around for a few days. I saw him getting out of a cab with two suitcases when I was coming back from the supermarket; so after I put the groceries away, I went over and knocked on his door."

Marritt was listening intently.

"There was some scurrying, at least it sounded that way; and then, about thirty seconds later, Doug let me in. I don't remember much about the conversation, but I remember looking up and seeing that one of the ceiling panels in the kitchen alcove was missing. I said something about it and he told me, 'Don't worry. I'm just doing some repair work.' Then he picked the panel up off the floor and fit it back into the ceiling. Now that I think about it, it didn't make much sense. All the repair work here is done by the super."

Marritt looked toward Dema, who was already on his feet. "Check it out," the detective ordered. Dema left the room on cue. His own supply of questions temporarily exhausted, Marritt leaned back against the couch. Aggy shifted position uncomfortably on the floor.

The rookie cop returned a minute or so later. "The panel's missing," he said. "I checked out the space above the ceiling. There's a big open area that someone lined with insulation. It's empty."

Marritt took a deep breath and let it out slowly. "Well, at least we've got a motive. Someone knew where he kept his money, or maybe his drugs, and someone killed him to get it."

Rubes sat up straight. "How much could it have been?"

The detective shrugged. "I don't know. That depends on how he spent his money and whether he kept it in the bank or at home. If he's been dealing for two or three years, it could have been anything from pigeon feed to a couple of hundred thousand dollars. I doubt he paid taxes on it."

Aggy sat silent.

Marritt stood up to leave. "One more question, Miss Tilden. "Have you slept at home every night for the past few weeks?"

"Yes."

"And you heard nothing?"

"No . . . At least, I don't think so."

"What does that mean?"

"Pardon?"

"What do you mean, you don't think so?"

"I don't understand."

The detective glowered. "Ten seconds ago, you said you didn't hear anything. Then you added 'at least I don't think so.' "

"So?"

"So, did you hear anything or not?"

"No."

Marritt shrugged. "All right. If you think of anything that might help, call me at the precinct house . . . You're *sure* there's nothing else you can think of?"

Aggy shook her head; then, as the cops were almost out the door, said something that Marritt didn't catch.

"He sure did," Dema told her.

“What’d she say?” Marritt asked the younger cop as they descended the stairs.

“She was just trying to be helpful.”

“Wonderful! Now answer my question. What did she tell you?”

“She said Doug Nicholas had a cat.”

CHAPTER 5

Still clad in pajamas, Matt leaned back on the sofa in his apartment and stretched his legs. Thanks to Christopher Columbus, born sometime in October on a day that Congress kept changing, he had the day off.

A wonderful gentleman, Matt thought of Columbus. Much more foresighted than Jesus or the Pilgrims when it came to planning a holiday. Thanksgiving and Christmas were complicated by family and friends. Generally, they were depressing as hell. Columbus Day was much simpler—no work, no family obligations and no strings.

Feet propped on the coffee table, Matt leafed through the morning newspaper. Toward the end of the first section, a small item caught his eye:

> THE POLICE BLOTTER
>
> A 31-year-old Manhattan man identified as Douglas Nicholas was found stabbed to death in his apartment at 366 West End Avenue yesterday afternoon. Police said that there were no clues in the slaying, which took place about three weeks ago.

Matt picked up the telephone and dialed Rubes's number. Three rings and a sleepy voice answered.

"It's Matt. Congratulations. I see in the *New York Times* that your girlfriend's apartment is about to be designated a city landmark."

Rubes rubbed his eyes. "Good news travels fast. What does the paper say?"

Matt read the article again, this time aloud.

"I called to tell you last night," Rubes said, "but you weren't in."

"I was in," Matt guffawed, "but I wasn't in a position to answer the phone, if you know what I mean."

"Yeah! Well, while you were having fun, I was being grilled by the cops."

Matt shifted position on the sofa. "Why you?"

"Well, it wasn't me, exactly. The cops were waiting when Aggy and I got back from the park, so I stayed while they talked with her."

"What do the police know about it?"

"Not much. They think it happened at night and whoever killed him knew where he kept his cash. Aggy told them he was a dealer, but she didn't hear anything."

"It sounds creepy," Matt said. "How's she taking it?"

"Pretty well, I guess. At least she was okay last night."

"Do I still get to meet her?"

"Sure, but let's hold off on it until Friday. That gives everyone a chance to calm their nerves."

"My nerves are fine."

"Your next-door neighbor didn't just get murdered," Rubes noted.

"Neither did yours," came the reply, "but that's okay. I'll see you Friday."

The conversation ended,. Rubes put down the receiver, picked it up again, and dialed Aggy's number. The BZST of a busy signal assaulted his ears. He put the phone down, went to the bathroom basin and washed his face, then came back and dialed again. Still busy.

"Maybe it's off the hook," he thought. Again, he dialed . . . BZST . . . BZST.

Rubes took off his pajamas. The phone rang.

"I hope I didn't wake you," said Aggy. "I just wanted to talk."

"How's the morning after?"

"Not so good," she told him. "But, boy, am I in love with Christopher Columbus. Give me liberty or give me whatever, just so I get the day off."

"Do you want company?"

"I guess so."

Rubes showered and dressed quickly, then walked a block to Broadway to pick up a Late City Edition of the *New York Times*. After reading the "Police Blotter" item, he turned back to the newsstand and bought a copy of the *Daily News*. There was no mention of the killing. For reasons unknown, the *News* had been scooped. Flipping the second paper in a trash can, he folded the *Times* under his arm and began walking back toward West End Avenue. On the sidewalk beneath a large plate-glass window, a gnarled old woman with shriveled black skin looked up at him and smiled. Two shopping bags piled high with personal belongings lay at her feet. As Rubes veered left to avoid her, she pointed to a large sign pinned to her coat. The sign read, "President Kennedy is alive in Cuba with the Communists."

Rubes kept walking. The sign bugged him. Hadn't she seen the goddamn pictures where the President's head was blown off? She couldn't even write a sensible sign. You couldn't tell from looking at it whether she meant Kennedy was being held captive or had joined the Communists. It didn't really matter. Didn't she know his whole goddamn head had been blown away?

The vestibule door at 366 West End Avenue was locked when Rubes arrived. Beside it, a message scrawled on coarse yellow paper warned:

> All Tenants! Because of murder, please lock door. Don't buzz in stranger.
>
> Dominick Calamari, Super.

Rubes pressed the appropriate intercom button and waited for Aggy's voice.

"It's me," he told her.

"Define me."

"Your ardent suitor and sometime breakfast companion."

A buzz sounded, and he pushed open the door, then climbed the stairs to the third-floor landing. Aggy was dressed in the same sweater and jeans she had worn the day before.

"I feel mortal," she announced, standing aside to let him in.

Rubes forced a smile. "Does that come as a surprise?"

"No, I just never thought about it before, and suddenly I feel very insubstantial. It frightens me a little."

"Do you want to talk about it?"

"Not particularly."

"I felt that way when my father died," Rubes offered. "The idea that I'd never see him again was outrageous. He'd kept every little thing I'd ever given him. There was a whole drawer full of junk—homemade birthday cards, pictures I'd painted in kindergarten, a ceramic hand print I'd made in first grade. That's when it hit home that I'd lost him."

The mannequin flashed through Aggy's mind.

"How well did you know him?" she heard Rubes ask.

"Huh?"

"How well did you know Doug Nicholas?"

"I said I didn't want to talk about it," she snapped.

"Okay; I'm sorry."

She shook her head, then suddenly stepped back. "That cop . . . The one who was here yesterday. What's his name?"

"Marritt," Rubes told her.

"Not him; the other one."

"I'm not sure. Dema, or something like that."

"That's it."

"Hey! Are you all right?"

"I've seen him," Aggy said.

"He's a cop. He's on duty around here all the time."

"That's not what I'm talking about."

"Hey," he asked a second time, "are you all right?"

Aggy blinked. "I guess so . . . At least I think I am. I'm sorry; I didn't mean to snap."

Protectively, he reached out to hold her. For a moment, she stood rigid. Then her legs weakened and she succumbed to his embrace, leaning forward and pressing her breasts against his chest.

"Hey! For a frightened woman, you're marvelously affectionate."

"Thanks."

"Would you like to make love?"

"I guess so."

The bed was unmade, sheets and blankets in disarray from the previous night. Almost as if he weren't there, Aggy lifted her sweater up over her head. Rubes unbuttoned his shirt and let it drop to the floor.

"Can I help with your bra?"

Removing it herself, she lay down on the bed, face up, with her jeans still on. As she did, her breasts melted into her chest, leaving two evenly shaped mounds.

Rubes lay beside her and began stroking her lacy black hair. "It's been a while," he said.

Again, the mannequin—this time, nude with a trickle of blood from its brow.

"You have a great body," he told her. "You know that, don't you?"

She didn't answer.

"And you're a wonderful lover."

Inside the kitchen alcove, a sharp-edged bread knife glistened in the sun. Rubes began caressing her breasts.

"I'm not in the mood," Aggy said, suddenly sitting up. "You'll have to stop."

"How come?"

"I don't know. I'm just not in the mood. I'm sorry."

Her eyes focused on a piece of molding near the crossbeam of the ceiling.

Rubes wondered if she was sleeping with anyone else.

"Don't worry," he told her. "It's the shock of realizing that everyone, including yourself, is mortal."

She wished he'd shut up.

"Once you've adjusted, it will be all right. No one lives forever."

"Can I add that to my list?" Aggy asked caustically.

Rubes nodded.

Shaking her head as though brushing away a bad dream, she rose from her bed and crossed to the kitchen alcove. There, tacked to the bulletin board, a neatly inscribed list read:

Tilden's Laws of Nature

1. If someone steals your umbrella, you're morally justified in stealing someone else's.
2. Anyone who can name the Seven Dwarfs in "Snow White" *and* the order in which they marched is a great American.
3. Cooked rice does not keep well in the refrigerator overnight.
4. Most men with waterbeds are assholes.
5. Children are allowed to call their parents collect. The converse does not hold true.
6. If someone offers you a Life Saver from a roll of assorted flavors, chances are they don't like the flavor they're offering and there's a red one coming up next.
7. Bears are great.

Very neatly at the bottom of the list, next to the spare set of keys on the bulletin board, she penciled in:

8. Agatha Tilden will not live forever.

Her mood, Rubes observed, was somewhat morbid.

CHAPTER 6

Police Lieutenant Richard Marritt arrived at the precinct house Wednesday morning in an unusually good mood. Thursday and Friday were his regular days off, and having given two pints of blood to the Red Cross in the preceding month, he was entitled to Saturday and Sunday as well. That meant he could paint the playroom, take the kids to a ballgame, and relax a little in between.

Passing through the precinct waiting room, he waved to the desk sergeant and bounded up the stairs to his office two at a time. He shared the room with six other detectives but, with staggered hours, there were seldom more than two of them in at once. Marritt liked the office. It set him apart from the patrolmen and gave him a bit of status. The cops pounding a beat had the R and R Room downstairs, but it was hard to get much rest and relaxation when eighty cops had access to a room not much bigger than a pool table.

Inside the office, Marritt pulled a pack of Marlboros from his shirt pocket and urged a cigarette from the crushproof box. Then, settling behind the shabby metal desk which stood at right angles with the far wall, he shoved the cigarette between his lips, lit it and inhaled.

It tasted lousy. He had managed to stay away from smoking for four months, and just last week started up again. Stubbing the cigarette out, he reached for the desk phone and buzzed the sergeant downstairs. "Send Dema up when he gets here."

Normally, a more seasoned cop—someone from the detective squad—would have been assigned to work with Marritt on the Doug Nicholas case. But Dema had asked for the job when the body was discovered and, with more satisfaction than the rookie realized, Marritt okayed the assignment. He liked Dema—liked him a lot. The kid had been on the force for less than a year, but he had a solid head on his shoulders. He kept his nose clean, and knew when to keep his trap shut. Like last Sunday afternoon over at Agatha Tilden's. Some cops would have spent the afternoon making small talk, trying to impress her. Dema stood there and took notes. He was good on details. Nothing eluded him, and he never tried to shove his way onto center stage when he didn't belong. Also, he was a hard worker. After all, it had been Dema who pushed Marritt into doing his job and answering the Doug Nicholas radio call in the first place.

"You wanted to see me, sir?"

Marritt looked up and saw the rookie cop in the doorway. Dema never barged in without permission either. That was another plus. Some patrolmen followed you up the stairs, talking at you the whole way, and barged into the detectives' office without an invitation. Dema knew his place. Maybe that was why Marritt treated him as something of an equal.

"Sit down. How's the world treating you?"

"Fine, sir."

Leaning forward, Marritt pushed the ashtray aside. He couldn't get away from feeling guilty about smoking, as though Dema, now sitting across from him, would know he had broken his pledge.

"I'm going to the ballgame this Sunday—Jets

against the Raiders," the detective said, not quite ready to concentrate on police work. "Are you a football fan?"

"Yes, sir."

"I'm a baseball fan myself," Marritt volunteered. "But it's played all wrong now. The game doesn't have any heart today. Changing cities . . . free agentry . . . artificial turf. Baseball should be played on grass. I remember when I was a kid. I'd ride the subway for an hour through dark dirty tunnels to get to Yankee Stadium. Then the tracks swooped out of the ground and this magnificent green diamond would be staring me in the eye. Real grass outdoors in the sun. Bleachers . . . hot dogs . . . peanuts. Now down in Houston they play under a roof in the Astrodome. God knows what they do in the rest of the country."

Dema nodded. Marritt shook his head. "Okay, I know it. I'm an old fogey and I'm boring you. Where do we stand on Doug Nicholas?"

"It looks like the girl was right," Dema answered. "He was a dealer. The apartment was pretty clean, but the lab found traces of grass, hash and cocaine above the kitchen alcove where the ceiling panel was missing."

"Anything else in the apartment?"

"A couple of things. Number one, I found a notebook with names, addresses and telephone numbers."

"Business or social?" Marritt asked.

"I'm not certain, but I doubt it's social. Some of the names are Spanish, and a few of the addresses are in Bedford-Stuyvesant and Harlem."

"I don't know if that means much," Marritt answered. "When it comes to dating, kids nowadays aren't that interested in color."

"Maybe not, but that brings us to item number two." For the first time, Marritt noticed the manila folder under Dema's right arm. "This is a chart I found in the bottom drawer of Doug Nicholas's desk. It lists all his sales and purchases; no names, but there are a lot of dates and dollar signs. It looks like he's been dealing for four years, and it looks like he made a lot of money."

"How much?"

"According to this chart, a profit of a quarter-million dollars."

A long whistle escaped Marritt's lips. "You're right. That's a lot of money. Do you know where he kept it?"

"Probably in the apartment. Item number three, I found his bankbook. It shows a balance of less than five hundred dollars, with virtually no entries over the past four years. There was no checkbook in the apartment, and the landlord says he paid his rent in cash. I ran a check with Central Credit. There's no other bank account registered under his name or social security number."

"That doesn't rule out an account under a false name."

"I know," Dema answered. "But that would have caused tax problems. I couldn't find a safe-deposit-box key either. I think someone killed Doug Nicholas for his money."

Marritt stared at the ceiling. Two hundred and fifty thousand dollars! That was more money than he had made in seventeen years as a cop. A quarter of a million dollars for knocking off some punk kid who no one even knew was dead for three weeks. Wordlessly, the detective opened a second folder that lay on the corner of his desk: "*Autopsy report—Douglas Nicholas:* Height—five feet eleven inches; weight—

one hundred sixty pounds; hair—brown; eyes—blue . . ." Turning to the next page, he read silently on: "The body is that of a white male approximately thirty years of age. There is advanced decomposition with brownish black discoloration of the skin. Gray mold is noted in a patchy distribution. Maggots are present in and on the surface of the body . . . All extremities intact; head and jaws in good condition . . . Traces of gonorrhea in blood samples and genitals . . . Death resulted from one or more of twelve stab wounds in the neck and upper body."

"He must have been a nut," Marritt said, returning the folder to its original corner of the desk. "What drug dealer in his right mind would keep records of sales and purchases?"

Dema didn't answer.

"Plus," the detective added, "with twelve stab wounds, it looks like he was killed by a nut. Maybe money wasn't the only motive."

"Why else would anyone do it?"

"Who knows? Passion; revenge. I've never understood guys who deal dope. Maybe that's because I don't smoke the stuff. . . . How about you?"

Dema looked up, startled.

"Just curious," the detective assured him. "It's not important. Half the cops in the precinct smoke. In fact, cops get the best grass in New York. All they do when they need it is find some long-haired kid walking down the street toking on a joint, shove him up against a wall, and confiscate his stuff. Then they say to him, 'All right! I ought to lock you up; but you seem like a nice kid, so I'll let you go!' The kid thinks he got off easy. Actually, all that happened is the cop lifted his grass."

Dema smiled nervously, and began to slide an index finger along a metal ridge on the arm of his chair. Marritt watched, embarrassed by the spot he had put the kid on. "It's all right," he said gently. "I'm not trying to cross-examine you. It's just, at my age, I've developed the habit of saying exactly what comes to mind." Even more embarrassed now by the fatherly affection he felt for the rookie, the detective pushed himself away from the desk, opened the middle drawer, and extracted a sheaf of papers he had been meaning to work on for several days. "Now get out of here. I have to push this file around to earn my salary."

Dema stood up and walked to the door, then stopped.

"You all right?" Marritt asked, looking up from the file.

"Yeah," Dema answered, nodding as he turned and passed out the doorway.

"Good work so far," Marritt called after him. "Except you forgot to deduct for living expenses. Based on that chart of yours, I think the person who killed Doug Nicholas didn't get more than two hundred thousand."

CHAPTER 7

Rubes was his usual one-man-welcoming-committee self when Matt arrived at his apartment Friday evening prior to dinner. Looking into the broad open smile and outstretched arms that confronted him, Matt couldn't help wondering whether his brother was really always that glad to see him. If so, the feeling wasn't mutual—not in degree anyway.

"It was Aggy's idea to cook dinner instead of going out," Rubes explained as they walked up West End Avenue. "She thought it would be more relaxing than going to a restaurant and you'd get to know each other better. That's all right, isn't it?"

Matt nodded. It wasn't all right, but he decided not to say anything. He should have known it would never be enough for Rubes if the three of them had a simple meal in a restaurant. Everything had to be a production. "She sounds nice," he said at last to hold up his end of the conversation.

"She is." There was an awkward silence. "I hope you like her."

Actually, Matt was in a relatively good mood. The pressure of the office had lifted for the weekend and his spirits, while not exactly soaring, were somewhat bolstered by the prospect of the weekend ahead.

Matt didn't like the office very much. After five years, the initial euphoria of working in a building that was a recognizable part of the Manhattan skyline had long since evaporated. He was tired of shuffling papers and taking orders from people who weren't as smart as he was. He didn't like going to lunch with superiors who drank too much while he stayed respectfully sober. With increasing frequency, he found himself sitting at his desk, looking out at the city, imagining himself an angry giant hundreds of feet tall toppling buildings and crushing bridges.

The walk to Aggy's was uneventful. At the concrete stoop, Rubes hit the buzzer and, moments later, they were inside. Aggy, as was her custom, was waiting in the doorway to her apartment, wearing unusually well-fitted jeans and a maroon ribbed sweater that accentuated her figure. Her black hair fell several inches below her shoulders.

"You're the first girl Rubes has gone out with who doesn't look like Anthony Quinn," Matt joked as he stepped inside.

Rubes's stomach tightened.

Aggy smiled.

"I understand you had some excitement here last weekend," Matt stated in matter of fact fashion.

Aggy stopped smiling.

"I'm sorry," he apologized. "I didn't mean to start on a down note."

Aggy took their coats and hung them in the closet.

"You have a nice apartment," Matt noted, seeking to recoup his losses. "How long have you lived here?"

"Two years."

"The plants are great. Which one do you like best?"

"The avocado. I suppose it's a little like a child. I planted the seed and watched it grow, and the bigger it gets, no matter what anyone else thinks, I love it."

Matt laughed. Rubes unwound a little more. His

brother was smiling and talking in animated fashion, which meant he liked Aggy. "I've never had much luck with plants," Matt admitted. "They always die on me."

"Try a begonia," she volunteered. "They're very hardy. Killing a begonia is a little like killing a rock. You can't do it."

"We've never gotten along too well with rocks in our family," Matt said with a smile. "Did Rubes ever tell you about the time when we were kids and he broke his toe?"

"No."

"Tell her," Matt urged.

"It isn't very interesting," Rubes mumbled. "We were playing touch football in the park and didn't have a kicking tee, so I put the ball up on a rock to kick off. You can figure out the rest."

Satisfied that his relationship with Rubes had been put in proper context, Matt settled on the sofa. Rubes sat on a chair by the window. Matt, he noticed, was wearing well-tailored cords compared to his own frayed-at-the-bottom jeans.

"Where are you from?" Matt asked, pursuing the conversation.

"Minnesota," Aggy answered. "About ten miles from Minneapolis."

"Are your parents still there?"

"Now and forever."

"What do they do for a living?"

"My father owns a hardware store. He's had it for twenty-five years. My mother's a part-time receptionist."

"And you?"

"I work at a day-care center in the Bronx."

Rubes edged his chair closer to the conversation.

"What about you?" Aggy asked, nodding in Matt's direction.

"I'm an account executive for Kronick & Rand. It's one of the oldline ad agencies."

"Do you like it?"

"It's all right." Shifting position on the sofa, Matt nodded toward the Confederate cavalry cutlass hanging on the far wall. "How often do you use that?"

"Every night, when I go to the delicatessen for a snack. It keeps away the muggers."

Add to the list of Agatha Tilden's assets the fact that she was an excellent cook. Dinner was shrimp scampi and salad. The difference between Aggy's scampi and the fare served in restaurants was that, with Aggy, there were enough shrimp. The salad included lettuce, mushrooms, artichoke hearts, avocados (not homegrown), croutons and blue cheese dressing.

When the meal was done, Matt helped clear away the dishes. "Are you planning your demise?" he queried, calling attention to the last of "Tilden's Laws of Nature" tacked up on the kitchen bulletin board.

"Not in the immediate future," Aggy answered. "But I have been a bit morose lately." Somewhat anxiously, she looked from one brother to the other. "Do you want some grass? I'm still a little tight about what happened across the hall. It might help me unwind."

"Is it good stuff?" Matt queried.

"Judge for yourself."

A large dark red candle stood on an end table near the fireplace. Leaving the kitchen alcove behind, Aggy turned off the lights, put the candle on the floor, and lit it. The wick caught fire and flamed upward. As it did, she took a small blue and white china canister from the same table and emptied its already rolled contents onto the floor.

"The last of Doug Nicholas's grass," she announced with a flourish, sitting cross-legged to form the third point of a human triangle.

Rubes bent forward, picked up a joint, and thrust its tip into the flame. The fire flared briefly, then subsided, leaving the wrapping paper charred at one end. Holding the joint between his lips, he sucked in and felt a surge of energy rush through his body. After five years of smoking, Rubes still had trouble defining what it was about the experience that he liked. Putting his thoughts into words left them flat. It was a little like trying to explain how a ham sandwich tasted. He couldn't do it. Matt was better with words. "I *saw* the notes Paul McCartney was playing on the bass," was how Matt had described the experience of being stoned. Matt had a gift for just about everything.

"What's the bracelet on your ankle?" Rubes heard his brother ask.

Aggy blushed. "It's my chastity belt. I used to think I'd be a virgin until I got married. Somewhere along the line, age seventeen to be precise, I changed my mind. That's when I got the ankle bracelet. It stays on until holy wedlock."

Matt laughed. Aggy was far prettier than any girl he might have imagined with Rubes, and he wondered if they were serious about each other. The joint changed hands . . . first to Aggy . . . then to Matt. Taking a drag, he stared into the candle.

"What do you think of heaven?" Rubes popped the question from left field.

Matt looked vaguely annoyed. "Why? Is this supposed to be it?"

Ignoring the comment, Rubes took another drag

on the joint. "If you could construct an afterlife, what would it be like?"

"You asked the question. What do you think?"

"I'm not sure," Rubes answered. "I was lying in bed one night and, well, it wasn't a dream. It was right before I fell asleep. I pictured a room, and I envisioned that when I die I'll be transported to that room until someone special I love dies and joins me. Like, suppose I'm in love and have a happy marriage and my life runs its course. Eventually, after death, my wife and I will be reunited in this room and, if we want, we can stay there for an eternity. All our physical needs will be fulfilled. Eventually though, we'll feel as though the life cycle has to go on. We'll say good-bye and, as we go out the door, we'll be picked up in a swirling maelstrom and whirled round and round until we stop turning and are reborn. It's a combination of heaven and reincarnation."

"Or like being locked in a closet," Matt added.

It was good grass. Rubes had smoked it before and, on the third drag, the pressures on his mind began to lift. Aggy's head was silhouetted against the wall. Rubes looked at her, then at the flame, then back into her eyes. Her mind was somewhere else, and the realization that she wasn't all there brought him down to earth. Again he was aware of Matt's presence, and he wished his brother weren't there. Matt was staring at Aggy intently.

"She's mine," Rubes thought to himself. "Back off."

"Hey," Matt asked suddenly. "If you sprinkle grass in the wax when you make a candle, will you get high when you burn it?"

No one answered. No one laughed. Matt shifted uncomfortably on the floor.

The joint passed in a circle three more times. Matt's eyes didn't move. Aggy's maroon ribbed sweater seemed tighter than before, and it was hard to tell whether or not she was wearing anything underneath. Rubes's thoughts were arching to the point where he could not attest to anything except maybe to the fact that he was very stoned.

"Hey," Matt coaxed, but Aggy didn't stir. She seemed hypnotized by the flame, her face rigid with concentration. He could see her ribs move as she took each breath.

The candle flamed higher, and a tiny stream of dark red wax began to spurt down its sides, splashing an uneven red pattern on the wooden floor. Aggy's eyes were wider now, filling with terror. The department-store mannequin flashed through her mind. It was pouring blood. A fiery sword flashed through the air. Her world was red. She was remembering a very brutal, violent dream she had experienced several weeks before . . . Only it wasn't a dream . . . She had heard it all. The violence . . . The murder . . . *She had been awake the night Doug Nicholas was killed. She had heard the whole thing.*

Aggy buried her head in her hands and began to shake. Matt reached out to steady her trembling body, but Rubes thrust a protective arm between them. He looked first at Matt, then at Aggy, who was shaking even more violently. "What's the matter?"

She didn't answer. Rubes staggered to his feet and turned on the lights. "What is it?"

She said nothing. Rubes took her by the shoulders and shook her harder than he meant to, then pulled her hands from her face. They were wet with tears and saliva. "What's the matter?"

She started to cry in short, irregular breaths.

"What is it?" Rubes repeated.

Aggy stared into the still-lit candle and bit down hard on the back of her hand.

"I heard it when Doug was killed."

Rubes's face went blank. "What do you mean? He was killed weeks ago, at night."

"You don't understand," she said. "I just remembered . . . Oh God, that sounds silly." Her voice rose. "I just remembered . . . I heard it all, and I suppressed it. I made myself forget."

"What are you saying?"

"I remember the buzzer and someone coming upstairs. It was late. It was three o'clock in the morning. And I remember Doug . . . I remember I heard fighting . . . and grunting . . . and there was blood, and he was stabbed over and over."

Rubes shivered. "Should I call the police?"

"Not yet," Matt interrupted. "We have to calm her down before we do anything."

No one spoke for what seemed forever. Rubes looked at Aggy, then to Matt. His brother was as pale as she was.

"What do you remember?" Matt asked.

There was no answer.

"We want to help you," he said in a low, level voice, "but we can't unless you talk to us. What did you hear?"

Still no answer. Matt snapped his fingers twice, and Aggy turned her face to the side.

Again, there was silence. Rubes reached into his pocket and pulled out a set of keys. "Take these," he said to his brother, "and wait for me at my apartment."

"I want to stay."

"It will be easier if you go. I'll come home when she's calmed down."

"But I can help."

"I doubt it."

"It doesn't make sense."

"Just do it."

Reluctantly, Matt reached for the keys, then stood up and crossed to the door. "Be careful with her," he said.

Rubes nodded, then turned back to Aggy. The color was completely gone from her face, and her head hung limp to one side. With as much firmness as he dared, he cupped her chin with his hand and lifted her eyes to the level of his.

"It's all right," he said, convincing no one. "No, it's not all right," he mumbled, "but it will be. Get hold of yourself."

Aggy pushed her chin to the side, and her head dropped. Rubes did nothing. Slowly, the heaving in her chest subsided, and she straightened to an upright sitting position on the floor.

"I'd like a glass of water," she said.

"Do you want ice?"

Stupid question. Who cared? Aggy didn't answer.

Rubes filled a large glass with tap water and handed it to her. Taking it with both hands, she drank in small measured sips, giving the glass back to him when she had finished.

"Do you want the rest?"

She shook her head.

"Do you feel better?"

She nodded.

Rubes smiled. "Can you talk about it?"

She nodded again.

"What do you remember?"

"I'm not sure. I remember someone coming upstairs. I don't know if I remember the buzzer or not. And I heard Doug let him in, and I remember Doug saying it was three o'clock in the morning."

"How do you know it was the night Doug was killed?"

"I heard more. I know I heard more."

"That's what you keep saying, but are you sure?"

"Yes."

"Are you sure?" Rubes repeated.

"Yes . . . No . . . I don't know."

He was leading her nowhere, and not doing it very well.

"I was afraid," she said. "I was asleep, and it woke me up, and I was afraid. That's all I remember."

"You said you heard Doug being stabbed. How can you hear someone being stabbed?"

"I don't know."

"The police said he was stabbed a dozen times. Is that what you remember?"

"I don't know . . . I heard a fight, and I was afraid."

"Are you afraid now?"

"Yes."

"Why?"

"Because I don't know what's inside me . . ." Again, tears . . . "I can't control my own mind."

Rubes handed her the glass of water and she finished what was left.

"Did you hear anyone besides Doug say anything?"

"I don't know."

"Did you hear a name?"

"I can't remember."

"What do you remember?"

"I don't know."

"What *do* you know?" he asked impatiently.

"I know I feel awful," she said. "And I feel guilty."

"That doesn't make sense."

No response.

"Why should you feel guilty?"

"I don't know."

"What's to feel guilty about?"

"I don't know," she shouted. And then her voice fell. "I feel . . . I feel like after the abortion."

Slowly, Rubes let his breath out. "Maybe that's it."

"Meaning what?"

"Look. You just said you feel like you did after the abortion. You feel guilty. Don't you think you might be mixing the abortion and the murder in your mind? You feel responsible for one death and now, to punish yourself, you're making believe you heard the other."

"I don't know."

"You keep saying 'I don't know.' All you do know is that you heard a buzzer you must have heard hundreds of times before and someone walking up stairs. You don't know what night you heard it, and all you remember about the murder is what the police told us last Sunday."

Aggy stared blankly.

"Right?" Rubes prodded.

"Maybe."

"Of course I'm right."

"I said *maybe,*" she screeched.

If she had a knife, Aggy told herself, she'd bury it in his stomach.

Again, Rubes was speaking. "Would you like me to spend the night?"

"Oh, Jesus! You've got to be kidding!"

"No, really! Wouldn't you feel better if I stayed?"

"I don't think so."

"Why not? You're awfully upset."

"I'll be fine."

"It's no problem, really. I'll be glad to stay. We don't have to make love."

"Your brother's at home waiting for you."

"That's not the point. Let me go pick up the keys from Matt. I'll tell him things are okay and be back in a few minutes." Gently, he reached out and touched her shoulder. "All right?"

Too weak to resist, Aggy nodded.

"Is that a yes?"

"Have it your way. It doesn't matter."

CHAPTER 8

By noon the next day, Aggy was alone. Rubes had managed to force his way back on Friday night and, as expected, had been an unwanted bore. She didn't want to talk about "it," and she didn't want her back scratched in bed. Finally, as the night wore on, he gave up trying and went to sleep.

"I wish you'd stop feeling so goddamn sorry for yourself," she told him as he slept. "It's all the time, and it never ends." Then, unable to blot out the sound of his breathing, she imagined herself an animal, lodged in a secure underground hole until, at last, fear succumbed to exhaustion. Then she too slept, waking periodically until morning when she sent him home. After that, Rubes called twice to find out how she was doing. Even Matt telephoned to see if she was all right.

"I'm fine," she told them. "It was just my imagination." But she wasn't "fine." Every noise made her jump. Even her nose was hallucinating. She kept smelling the scented candles that Doug used to burn in his apartment. "They're aphrodisiacs," he had once told her, laughing as he said it. But she was unable to get the smell out of her nostrils, and blowing into a handkerchief only made it worse.

Finally, in near desperation, she seated herself at the kitchen table, paper and pen in hand. There were letters to write, lists she could make to take her mind off her problems. But the pen kept clotting. It smudged the paper, and in frustration Aggy hurled it across the room and watched it skittle under the bed. Then, from the corner of her eye, she saw something move. Looking over to prove that it was only her imagination, she saw a huge roach crawling across the table toward her.

"Get out of my house," she screamed, slamming the insect again and again with her fist. "Get out of my goddamn home." And then, hearing herself scream, she was frightened by her lack of control. Right then, she resolved there would be no more visions. Whatever she had heard on the night of the murder, real or imagined, there was nothing more that could be done. She wouldn't become involved in the depths of something that was over and which she didn't understand.

The rest of the day dissolved in a fit of cleaning. She scrubbed floors and washed walls, repotted a half dozen plants and cleaned the shower curtain with a passion. "Why are bathroom tiles always so ugly?" she wondered as she scoured porcelain niches around the sink. Through it all, the radio blared—Kenny Rogers, John and Yoko, Barbara Mandrell.

And then it was night. And, again, Rubes called. "How are you?" he asked for the third time that day.

"Holding together."

"What did you do this afternoon?"

"Cleaned house; repotted some begonias." As the conversation progressed, Aggy made a mental tally of Rubes's good points: "Number one, he's loyal. That's a plus. He's not stupid. He likes me a lot—that has its pluses and minuses."

"By the way," she queried. "Do you know what happened to Doug's cat?"

"Not really . . . Hey!" Rubes said suddenly, his

voice rising in mock anticipation. "Maybe that's the missing clue." He chuckled as the idea caught on in his mind. "Yeah, the cat probably had the key to a safe-deposit box tied around its neck."

Aggy didn't answer.

"All right. You don't like that theory. How about this one? Maybe the cat was really just a doll and the money's inside it. Then—"

For a moment, Aggy thought she'd hang up and call the telephone company to get her number changed. "Rubes," she interrupted, "forget it, okay. It was a silly question."

"I'm just trying to cheer you up," he said with a modicum of hurt.

"I appreciate it, but it's late and I'm tired. Good night."

With those words, she hung up, then turned on the television and began to fidget. The apartment was oppressive, and she didn't want to be there. Too many unpleasant things had happened indoors lately. She didn't like the brownstone anymore. It no longer seemed quaint. Its crumbling façade and dark corridors were portents of doom. The multicolored plants that ringed her apartment were losing their battle against the more ominous public halls.

Taking a jacket from the closet, Aggy opened the front door and ventured down the narrow corridor, double-locking the door behind her. She wanted to be outside where she could walk. On the street, the cool night air swept over her, and she began to feel better.

The murder was bizarre. "Things like this don't happen to people like me," she told herself. "Maybe to other people from other homes, but not to Agatha Tilden from Minnesota." Reaching Broadway, Aggy turned north. "Murder," she thought. "It's a funny word"—the first legal term she remembered learning as a child, one of the absolutes. "I murder, you murder, he murders," she chanted. "Commits murder, the crime of murder, the murdered . . . Jesus," she scolded herself. "Cut it out."

She wondered why Rubes had vetoed the idea of calling the police to tell them what she remembered, or had it been Matt? Either one, it didn't matter. Something in the way Dema had looked at her that afternoon in her apartment, before his eyes turned away, had been sufficient warning—a sign of recognition, an admonition that said, "Lady, don't get involved!"

86th Street . . . 90th . . . On the corner of Broadway and 96th, Aggy realized that her destination would be the Columbia-Barnard campus. "Those were happier times," she told herself. Besides, the late-night student hangouts would still be active and, even four years later, she might find a familiar face or two.

The neighborhood had changed. As Aggy neared the campus, she realized that the places she had frequented most were no longer there. One had been replaced by a fast-food joint. All that remained of another was a cracked front window and a sign which said Premises For Rent.

"Please let The Oak Bar still be here!"

On the corner of Broadway and 112th Street, Columbia's oldest student watering hole looked the same as ever. Stepping inside, Aggy removed her coat and glanced around. Tiny tables lined the walls, but the center of activity was still the huge, oval bar in the middle of the room. Made of solid oak, it dwarfed the students and teaching assistants who stood around it. The crowd was younger than she remembered it being, but Aggy knew it hadn't changed. She was just older.

"Can I join you?"

Aggy looked up at the bespectacled man who had moved to her side. He was a shade over six feet tall, well built, with curly brown hair and not bad-looking except for the dark-rimmed glasses perched on his nose.

"Can I join you?" he asked again. "My name is Paul Norman."

She smiled. "My name is Aggy."

He smiled back. "That's an unusual name."

"It's short for Agatha. My parents thought that suffering would make me a better person."

He laughed. "Were you named after Saint Agatha?"

"Who?"

"Saint Agatha. She was an early Christian martyr, sometimes portrayed with a salver holding her severed breasts."

"And that," Aggy told herself, "is what I get for trying to be witty with an academic."

"Are you a student?" he asked.

"Not anymore. I graduated four years ago."

"From Barnard?"

"Right."

"What brought you up here tonight?"

"I felt like walking." She was also getting tired of answering questions. "What about you? Do you live around here?"

"On 114th Street. I'm a Teaching Assistant at Columbia."

"What kind of course?"

"Philosophy."

"A perpetual Ph.D. candidate?"

"I guess so," he answered.

Aggy looked him over. She had meant to be glib, but was bordering on bitchy. "My freshman year of college," she announced, moderating her tone, "I only dated philosophy majors. I was convinced they knew the secret of life."

Paul Norman grinned. "Do you have a boyfriend?"

"Kind of."

"What does that mean?"

"Could I have a beer?" she countered.

"Sure."

The mugs were still the same. Thick opaque glass with a Columbia insignia etched on the side. They had two beers each. "I've got to go," Aggy said as she finished beer number two.

He looked her over from top to bottom. "Would you like to get together for dinner sometime?"

"I guess so."

"I'll need your telephone number."

"Why don't you give me yours instead," she said. "I'll call when I'm free."

"Is that a brush-off?"

"No, really. I'll call when I'm ready."

"Are you in the phone book?"

"Look, Paul," she answered. "Forget it, okay? Just leave me alone. That's all I want."

One o'clock . . . one-thirty . . . Aggy kept walking. Sometime after two, somewhere on Broadway, a tall, shapely woman stepped from the shadows and moved past her. The woman was attractive. Light-skinned, Hispanic, with a long purple dress and long black hair. As Aggy watched, she advanced on an older man and led him by the arm back into the shadows. The man was black and about fifty. He limped noticeably and bore the signs of too much liquor over too many years. "Oh baby," Aggy heard him say to the woman. "I don't got that kind of money . . . Wait

. . . Please . . . I'll give you two dollars if you let me walk down the street with my arm around you."

They left the shadows together—his arm drawn tight around her shoulders, her arm curved above his waist. Aggy watched as they vanished into the night.

CHAPTER 9

Richard Marritt arrived at the precinct house Sunday morning at ten o'clock. Dema's face registered surprise.

"I know I said I was going to the football game," the detective growled, pouring himself a cup of coffee, "but this murder is bugging me. There's something that doesn't fit." Still grumbling, he poked through the boxes and jars surrounding the coffee pot. "Where's the goddamn sugar?"

"It's gone," Dema told him.

"Christ," the detective muttered, filling his cup to the brim with powdered artificial cream. "Anyway, remember last year there was an article in the paper about some guy in Topeka, Kansas, who murdered two preachers and a nun. And after he was arrested, the police went to his house and found five thousand Gideon Bibles in the attic. Well, there's something screwy here too."

"I'm not sure I see the analogy, sir. I mean with the Gideon Bibles."

"Screw the analogy. It isn't very good. I wanted to sleep late this morning and then go to the football game, but I couldn't because this case is bugging me."

Sitting behind his desk, Marritt nudged the wastepaper basket closer with his foot, then watched in dismay as it overturned, spilling papers, cigarette butts and ashes onto the floor. "Let it lie there," he ordered as Dema bent forward. "I'll pick it up myself later." Reaching into his pocket, he took out a pack of cigarettes and offered one to the younger man.

"No thanks," Dema told him. "I don't smoke."

"Neither should I, but I do." Marritt took a shlurp of unsweetened coffee, then turned his head back toward the rookie. "What have you found out about Doug Nicholas since Wednesday?"

Dema opened his manila folder and scanned the notes on page one. "I've interviewed half the people in his address book, and they all say the same thing. He dealt on his own. He sold grass, hash and coke. It was good stuff, relatively low-priced. He bought it in Texas, flew it back to New York on regularly scheduled airlines, and sold it to anyone who had the money to buy. Sometimes he sold out of his apartment, sometimes on the street. He never said much about the size of his business, and almost everyone I talk with is surprised to hear how big his operation was. He dealt strictly in cash."

"There's a piece of cork panel missing from the ceiling above the kitchen alcove," Marritt noted sarcastically. "Did anyone have anything to say about that?"

"No, sir."

"Did he have any friends, anyone in particular that he trusted?"

"Not that I've been able to find out. But there was no sign of forced entry into the apartment, so he must have let in the person who killed him. After that, who knows."

Swiveling in his chair, Marritt reached out with his foot for the overturned wastepaper basket and pulled it closer. That done, he stretched out a leg and rested it gently on the basket rim. "Don't worry about it," he told the rookie, who was looking at the trash on the linoleum floor. "It won't bite."

"I'm sort of an old maid about some things," Dema confessed.

"You and my wife would get along great." Marritt nodded toward the pile. "Be my guest if it makes you happy."

Dema rose from his chair and began putting the trash back in the basket. As he did, Marritt's thoughts returned to the kitchen alcove. "Where's the ceiling panel, and why is it missing?"

"Maybe the killer took it with him."

"Why?"

"Fingerprints?"

"No way," the detective answered. "There weren't any fingerprints in the apartment. None on the door. None on the bureau. The killer must have worn gloves."

"Maybe he took them off to pry open the panel."

Marritt gritted his teeth. "It still doesn't make sense. He could have wiped the panel clean."

"Not if there was a lot of noise. Don't forget. It was a slow, sloppy killing. He might have been afraid the police were coming."

"I suppose that's right," Marritt conceded. "The panel isn't there now anyway. He must have taken it with him. Unless . . . unless someone cleaned up after him."

"I don't understand."

"Use your imagination. Suppose one person killed Doug Nicholas—maybe a buyer who was all doped up and looking for a fight, or some broad he'd been screwing. And then someone else comes along, finds the body, and latches onto the money."

"I don't see the evidence for that."

"Right now, there's evidence for nothing," the detective grumbled.

Dema finished pushing the cigarette butts into a

neat pile and lifted them into the basket with a piece of paper.

"Gimme the case file," Marritt ordered.

The young cop complied.

"Okay," the detective exhorted. "Let's take a look at what we've got. What did we find in the room with the body? First, there was the normal stuff—books, clothes, phonograph records. For the time being, let's discount all of that. Next, there was a headless cat—also not much help. But we also found the victim's watch and wallet, right out in the open on the desk. That means we're not dealing with a random burglar. Regardless of who killed Doug Nicholas, whoever stole the money knew what they were looking for. He, or she, didn't bother with the small stuff."

Dema waited until he was sure Marritt had finished. "I'm not quite sure where all that gets us."

"Not very far," the detective muttered. "In case you're wondering, good police work is about ten percent inspiration, ten percent perspiration, and eighty percent luck. We need some luck." Wordlessly, he began to thumb through Doug Nicholas's little black address book, voicing random observations as he went. . . . "Kiner . . . Synodinos . . . Premanjeli Benzavit—Christ, what a name . . . Kunen . . . Murphy . . . Hey! Here's one!" he announced. "Reuben, Matt; three-ten East Sixty-ninth Street. What does he have to say about this mess?"

"I haven't talked to him yet."

"Well, when you do, find out if he's related to the boyfriend—the one who was with Agatha Tilden when we found the body."

"And if he is, so what?"

"I don't know," Marritt grumbled. "But something strange is going on here, and I'm curious. If ever a case stank, this is it. . . . And that's another thing," he said, suddenly pounding his fist on the desk. "That girl across the hall—our friend, Miss Tilden. There was a dead body next door to her for three weeks. The corridor stunk. She must have smelled it."

"Probably."

"You're damn right, probably. And I'll tell you something else. This was not a quiet killing. She should have heard it."

"Maybe she was out."

"She said she slept at home every night this month. I asked her."

"It could have happened early in the evening before she got home," Dema argued. "Besides, her boyfriend was there when you questioned her. What would you expect her to say if she was two-timing him?"

Marritt drummed his fingers on the desk. "It doesn't make sense. What's she hiding from us?"

"Are you sure she's hiding something?"

"Of course I'm sure," the detective answered. "There was a rotting, maggot-infested body across the hall for three weeks, and she says she didn't smell it. Doug Nicholas was hacked to pieces, sometime at night according to the melted-down candle on the bureau, and she says she didn't hear it. He was her neighbor for Christ's sake. They lived on the same floor of a small brownstone building. The fact that she didn't see him for three weeks should have been enough to make her suspicious." He paused. "What are the chances that Agatha Tilden was sleeping with Doug Nicholas?"

"Very slim," Dema answered, "based on what I've found out about him. Besides, she told us he wasn't her type."

"That's not enough to rule out the possibility that

they were lovers," Marritt pressed. "And, if they were, it gives us a motive. In fact, it gives us several motives. Possibility number one is that she killed him for his money."

Dema's eyes belied his skepticism. "I didn't think a woman could hack a man up like that."

"That's because you haven't been around long enough. A woman can do anything a man can do, sometimes better. And then there's possibility number two. Maybe she had help."

"The boyfriend?" Dema queried.

"Maybe. Or maybe the boyfriend killed Doug Nicholas out of jealousy, and someone else took the money. The possibilities are endless. One thing I *can* tell you—she's holding out on us. I want you to put her name through every computer we have. Get all the information you—"

Breaking off in mid-sentence, Marritt looked down at a giant water bug that was wending its way across the floor. Wordlessly, he lifted his foot and stomped down hard with the heel of his shoe.

"You have no heart," Dema said with a smile, scooping up the remains of the crushed insect with a piece of paper and dropping it in the basket.

"Yes I do," the detective growled. "But it's a black one."

CHAPTER 10

Monday, Aggy decreed, was to mark the resumption of business as usual. But the kids at the day-care center made it rough. They were more obstreperous than usual, particularly the older ones and especially Benjamin. Four and a half was old enough to be in kindergarten. The kid could be a pain in the neck.

"Gimme my goddamn crayons . . . Cut it out . . . Eat it."

Maybe the abortion hadn't been such a bad idea.

"Miss Tilden?"

"Yes, George?"

"Is it true that white people can't go potty unless they have a newspaper with them?"

From Benjamin. "Yeah! They get constipated. It's psychological or something."

From Aggy. "Fiddlesticks!"

"What does fiddlesticks mean?"

"It means bullshit," Benjamin offered.

Teaching jobs were hard to come by, she reminded herself, and day-care work paid the bills.

From Benjamin. "Get out of my seat, Wanda, or I'll smash you."

From Aggy. "Benjamin, I thought I taught you to be polite."

"*Please* get out of my seat, Wanda, or I'll smash you."

Who could tell. Maybe the kids would perform

better in school next year because Aggy had worked with them.

"Hey," Benjamin shouted indignantly, emerging from the bathroom. "Who forgot to flush the toilet?"

After work, Aggy walked down Columbus Avenue. The street was loud and dirty; no trees; nothing green. Just an endless convoy of long gray trucks rumbling by on cracked asphalt that would worsen with the winter ahead. The wind blew trash along the sidewalk and soot into her eyes. Turning her face to the side, Aggy caught a glimpse of her reflection in the window of a small plant store and, after a moment's hesitation, stepped inside. There, she was largely ignored by the proprietor and left to wander through the tightly packed plants on the shabby floor. Choosing a small begonia, she paid at the door and, out on the street, reexamined her acquisition. One slightly yellowed leaf stood out among the green. "Death among the living," she told herself. Or, to be less dramatic, the yellow leaf looked "yucky." She broke it off and tossed it on the sidewalk. "I'll probably get arrested for littering," she thought. "That's a laugh. Arrested for littering leaves. Cigarette butts and orange peels are okay, but leaves are verboten." She was unusually depressed. "It's a dirty city," she thought to herself. "The streets are filthy. No, that's not fair. There's no such thing as a dirty city. It's the people who live here."

Up ahead, three teenage boys just past the age of puberty leaned against a parked car. "Hey, baby," one of them grunted as Aggy walked by, "I want to fuck you."

"What's the matter," she shot back without breaking stride. "Your mother busy?"

Two points for a clever remark—but the incident irked her and, by the time she arrived home, she was even more depressed. The apartment seemed empty and her collection of plants somehow pathetic. "My children," she said under her breath, setting the new begonia on the fireplace mantel. Who was it who had said that about her plants? Maybe it had been Doug.

There were leftovers for dinner. She ate; read; turned the television on, then off again. The kids at the day-care center were on her mind. She'd thought about them a lot lately—and her younger self. When she was little she'd wanted long hair; but she wouldn't comb it, so her mother had made her wear it short. Once as a present, Aggy, age five, had picked flowers for her parents from a neighbor's garden. Her mother slapped her in the face. "It wasn't my fault. I didn't know I was stealing flowers."

At midnight, Aggy went to bed, and the wind began to swirl. As it grew in intensity, the leaded windows beside her bed rattled and danced and heavy drops of rain dotted the panes. Across the hall, there was moaning. Aggy's eyes closed tighter. She was lying in menstrual blood that poured down the inside of her thighs, across her legs, and through the runnels between her toes. The noise grew louder and Doug crashed against the door. "It's three o'clock in the morning," he laughed. "Don't you know better than to come here at three o'clock in the morning? You'll wake the whole building."

"Stay asleep," something inside warned. "Stay asleep! Make it a dream."

The next night—Tuesday—the forms came again. Two of them . . . "What are you doing here?" . . . There was silence . . . "What do you want?" . . .

Aggy's eyes fixed on the hands in front of her. Blood spurted from an altar on the floor.

"Go away," she shouted. "Leave me alone."

"Sacrilege," a voice cried.

Very gently, hands trembling, Aggy placed a child on the altar. "The dagger," she asked. "Where is it?"

"In your hand," the voice answered.

"Thank you." Aggy brushed a strand of hair from her forehead. "It won't be long now."

Holding the dagger level with her eyes, she gripped the handle, then plunged it downward into the child's heart. Again and again . . . again and again . . . until she lost consciousness.

And then she was awake, and alone, a cold sweat chilling her body. "Careful now," Aggy said to herself. "Don't lose control."

She climbed out of bed and pulled a robe tight around her shoulders. In the kitchen alcove, she slipped the cellophane off a box of English muffins and pushed both halves of a muffin into the toaster. When they reappeared, she spread a slab of butter across them and watched it flow like molten lava into the craters of the moon.

"I'm not crazy," she told herself. "I'm not crazy; I'm not!"

But there was no way she was going back to bed. Instead, she sat by the large bay window, waiting for the dawn. And when it came, she remembered the piece of paper they'd given her at the abortion clinic, the one with the name and number of a psychiatrist written down. She'd saved it, somewhere. And when she ferreted through the side pocket of her handbag, it was there—"W. N. Hoffmann, 44 West 63rd Street, 225-3011."

She sat for several minutes with the paper in her hand, wondering why she was about to do something she had never considered before. Then, slowly, she dialed Dr. Hoffmann's number. Two rings, and a metallic-sounding voice answered: "Hello. This is Dr. Willis Hoffmann, and you're talking to a telephone answering machine. When you hear the beep, please leave your message along with a number where you can be reached. I will call you back as soon as possible. In case of emergency, please call—"

"Fuck! I don't need this!"

Offended by the indignity of it all, Aggy slammed down the receiver and crumpled the paper in her hand.

The day passed. Rather than go to work, she called in sick, then slept. Midway through the afternoon she awoke, relatively rested and refreshed. What to do? The "Witchcraft, Magic and Sorcery" course flyer, still on her desk, caught her eye . . . "That's right; tonight at the museum; lecture number one . . . I'll go," she decided. Somehow, her fears always seemed to dissipate in the light of something new to do.

"Maybe I'm a little nuts," she said aloud, "but I can still function. And for the moment, I'm hungry." Rummaging through the kitchen cupboard, she found a jar of peanut butter and put it on the counter. "Shit," she grumbled a moment later. "No black raspberry jam. How can anyone run a home without black raspberry jam?"

Rubes called just after seven to say hello.

"Listen," he announced. "If you feel up to it, I'd like you to come with me to Princeton this weekend. The Columbia-Princeton football game is Saturday, and since Matt went to Princeton, it's a family rivalry. Princeton always wins, which is very frustrating, but it's fun anyway."

"Just what I want," she answered without enthusiasm.

"It would mean a lot to me," Rubes pressed. "Besides, it's just for the day, and Matt's bringing some blonde he's hot about. You could check her out and give me an expert opinion on her personality and looks."

"What's her name?"

"I don't know. I've never met her, but Matt says her kisses are so wet he needs one of those things the dentist puts in your mouth to drain the saliva. And she has big tits."

"Rubes, how would you like to change the subject?"

"Say yes; please; just this once."

He begged and pleaded until finally she weakened. "All right! I'll go."

"Okay! And one more thing. It's about Doug Nicholas."

Aggy tensed.

"Last Friday night, when you started to remember—"

She didn't want to hear it. "Rubes, I have to go. I've got a course at the museum in twenty minutes. If I stay on the phone any longer, I'll be late."

She left for the museum minutes later and, on arriving, walked slowly toward the front gate. By day, the building appeared drab and lifeless, its colorless stone walls blending with the environment. By night though, it assumed a different aura, far more like the centerpiece of a Gothic novel than a repository of national learning. Gazing toward the tallest of its towers, Aggy noted a solitary light ablaze through a narrow window. "The ghost of Margaret Mead is no doubt working late tonight," she romanticized.

Winding her way past a statue of Theodore Roosevelt on horseback, Aggy entered the museum and found the lecture hall without difficulty. Some forty persons had preceded her into the room, and she surveyed them with a modicum of disappointment. About half were women. None of the men were good-looking. No one sparked her interest. Taking a seat midway down the center aisle, she reached into her pocketbook for a stick of gum and glanced around, oblivious to the figure sliding into the chair beside her.

"Aren't you going to say hello?"

Aggy jumped. "What are you doing here?"

Matt grinned. "I saw the course catalogue on your desk the night Rubes and I were over at your place for dinner. To be honest, I didn't know the museum gave courses, but the idea of learning how to spin straw into gold intrigued me."

A slender, rather hungry-looking man dressed in a gray pinstripe suit walked to a lectern in front of the room and cleared his throat. "Welcome," he said in an unduly somber tone.

"An inspiring opening line," Aggy thought. "I wonder what comes next?"

The room fell silent, and the lecturer began: "We begin this evening a sociological inquiry into the foundations of witchcraft, magic and sorcery. These terms have been used to connote varying acts and practices throughout the ages. For our purposes here tonight, we will define them as a class of actions and beliefs related to the control of events and one's environment through reliance upon the supernatural."

Two rows in front of Aggy and Matt, a hand shot into the air. "Could you tell us, sir, what you mean by 'supernatural'?"

"Certainly. Supernatural may be defined as something that is outside the accepted established order; something that one can only express a belief with reference to. However, we must not lose sight of the fact that something which is regarded as supernatural in one society might be fully tangible in another. For example, tape recorders, cameras and guns—all instruments known by us to operate on fundamental physical principles—might be thought of as supernatural in another society."

Aggy took a small pad from her purse and began to doodle. She had always thought it would be fun to spend a night in the Museum of Natural History, but this wasn't what she had in mind. Professor Pinstripe never used a monosyllabic word where a polysyllabic substitute was available. In private conversation, he no doubt used "pusillanimous" instead of "cowardly."

"One either is or is not a witch," the instructor went on. "It is not a voluntary state of being. By contrast, sorcery is a technique. Unlike witchcraft, it entails acquired skills, and one who is a sorcerer has attained his status by choice."

Matt looked down at Aggy's pad. In large capital letters, she had written "RUBES/MATT" at the top of the page. Below that, in lower case, she penciled in "Doug."

". . . Who is to say whether a set of beliefs constitutes religion or witchcraft, magic and sorcery. Both deal with the supernatural. Religion, however, is supplicative in nature. It seeks help from and the blessings of God. Witchcraft, magic and sorcery, on the other hand, are manipulative and involve a far greater degree of self-help."

Aggy continued to doodle, spelling out "LIVED" in large capital letters in the middle of the page. Absentmindedly, she circled the word and ran an arrow through it to one of the brothers' names.

The voice droned on.

"For all witchcraft, a victim is required, and the traditional relationship between the accused, the accuser and the alleged victim supports the view that, over the ages, most allegations of witchcraft have been motivated by personal malice or broader social, political and economic ends."

Matt pulled a thin leather memo pad from an inside jacket pocket and drew a gallows in the center of the page. Beneath that, he wrote "Names of Places" and inscribed ten dashes for letters. That done, he touched Aggy on the arm and pointed to the pad. "Hangman?" he queried.

"I don't see why you came if you're not interested in listening," she whispered harshly.

"You're not so attentive yourself, Goody Two Shoes."

Someone touched Matt on the shoulder from behind. He glared and fell silent.

"For example," the instructor continued. "A classic case of so-called witchcraft emanated from the Lugbara tribesmen in Central Africa . . ."

"Would you like a cup of coffee?" Matt asked when the class ended.

"I don't like coffee."

"That was a figure of speech," he explained with exemplary patience, closing up the leather memo case and slipping it back into his pocket. "You can have a Coke if you'd like."

Aggy hesitated. There was no sense in being unfriendly. "Okay," she said at last. "I'd like some ice cream."

"Fine. This is your neighborhood. Where should we go?"

They walked several blocks to a glass-enclosed sidewalk café and took seats away from the door to avoid the draft.

"Don't look now," Matt warned when they were seated, "but there's a spider crawling up your leg."

Aggy glanced downward. "I don't see it."

Matt leaned forward and plucked a tiny arachnid from her jeans, dropping it lightly on the floor.

"You're more humane than I thought," she said. "I would have expected you to stomp on it."

Matt laughed. "I never kill spiders. After all, along with pigeons and roaches, they're part of New York's indigenous wildlife."

Aggy smiled. The waitress arrived, and she ordered a chocolate sundae, Matt a hamburger and Coke.

"I see you're one of the lucky few who don't have to count calories," Matt joked.

"Is he making a pass at me?" Aggy wondered. "Probably not! . . . Why not? Because he doesn't want to give me the satisfaction of turning him down . . . Would I? You bet your ass."

"I suppose I should diet," she answered, "but it's too much of an effort. Besides, dieting is like being celibate. I don't have much taste for either."

The waitress put two glasses of water on the table along with a relish tray and a bottle of ketchup. Matt sneezed. "God bless you twice," Aggy proclaimed.

"Why twice? I only sneezed once."

"I know, but a person never sneezes just once. Sneezes always come in groups of two or more."

Matt sneezed again.

"I told you so," she said triumphantly.

The waitress reappeared with their food. Matt took a bite of pickle.

"Down the hatch," Aggy said cheerfully, preparatory to her own first bite.

"Enjoy."

"Oh, my God," she thought suddenly. "What if Rubes sees us here? If he walks by this window now, he'll die."

CHAPTER 11

Rubes stood in the kitchen and contemplated the remains of his dinner. Grilled cheese sandwiches weren't fancy, he told himself, but they made an okay meal. They were easy to cook, tasted good, and necessitated a minimum of cleaning up afterward. Carefully, so as not to let the residue of burnt cheese fall to the floor, he crumpled the used piece of tinfoil and tossed it in a container of garbage by the stove. With one act of domesticity, the kitchen was clean.

It was nine o'clock, which meant Aggy wouldn't be home from the museum for at least an hour, and he didn't feel like reading. For lack of anything better to do, he wandered into the tiny bedroom and turned on the television. Switching stations until his options were exhausted, he turned the set off, then decided on impulse to take a walk. October was almost over, and November in New York was always cold. He might as well walk while he could enjoy it. Just as he was reaching for his coat, the doorbell rang.

"Coming," he announced.

Opening the door, Rubes faced Detective Richard Marritt.

"I'd like to talk with you, Mr. Reuben."

"Sure, come on in."

Not content simply to step inside, Marritt walked past the kitchen alcove to the middle of the living room.

"Would you like a seat?"

"No thanks," the cop answered draping his overcoat on the living-room sofa. "I've been on my butt most of the day. I'll stand."

"Minor problem," Rubes thought. "Does this mean I have to stand too, or can I sit . . . Hell, it's my apartment . . . I'll sit."

Marritt watched as his host was seated, then did likewise. "I changed my mind," he announced. "That's a cop's prerogative."

Rubes smiled awkwardly.

Marritt looked around. "Nice place you have here." (Actually, he thought it sucked.) "How much does it cost?"

"Three fifty a month."

"Not bad, considering today's rent market."

There was something vague in the way the apartment had been put together—characterless, was how the detective saw it. Battered chairs that had passed via garage sales and block parties. A splintered bookshelf that looked as though it had been picked up off the street.

"Where do you work, Mr. Reuben?"

"I teach sixth grade."

"I didn't ask what you did. I asked where you did it."

"P.S. 145 in the Bronx."

Marritt rubbed his forehead with the back of his hand. "I'm sorry," he said. "I didn't mean to jump on you. One of my kids was up at five this morning with the flu. It's been a long day and I'm working overtime. What do you teach?"

"Math."

"Is that the new math?"

"Yes, sir."

"I figured as much. If you'll forgive my saying so,

I think the new math is a lot of crap. Kids don't learn how to add and subtract anymore, just a lot of gobbledygook about sets and number theory. Take it from me, in five years, the old math will be back in fashion."

"Maybe so," Rubes answered affably.

"You're damn right, maybe so."

The detective looked around, continuing to assess the apartment—a small table, cheap sofa, peeling paint on the ceiling and walls. "What do you know about Doug Nicholas?" he asked at last.

"Not much."

"I didn't ask how much; I asked what."

Rubes shrugged. "I know he was a dealer."

"Did you ever meet him?"

"Not formally. We passed each other now and then in the corridor outside Aggy's apartment. I may have nodded hello."

"Did you ever buy from him?"

"No, sir."

"What about your girlfriend?"

"I think she bought from him once or twice."

"What was the nature of their relationship?"

"So far as I know, they were neighbors, nothing more."

"Did they ever date one another?"

"Not that I know of."

"Are you sure of that?"

"No."

"Can you think of any reason why she might not want to be completely honest with us about the killing?"

The questions were beginning to make Rubes uncomfortable.

"You haven't answered my question, Mr. Reuben. Can you think of any reason why your girlfriend might not want to be completely honest with us?"

"No, sir."

"Then why did it take you so long to answer?"

"I was considering the matter fully to give you an honest answer."

"And?"

"I can't think of any reason."

"Does she have any money problems?"

"No."

"Does she go out with other guys?"

"I don't know . . . I guess so . . . I mean, I assume she has other men friends."

"How often do you see her?"

"Once or twice a week."

"When you spend the night together, is it at your place or hers?"

It was an outrageous question and Marritt knew it, but he was confident Rubes wouldn't object.

"Her place," came the answer.

"It figures," the detective told himself. "It's obvious who the dominant one is in this relationship."

It was time to break new ground. "Mr. Reuben, do you have any brothers or sisters?"

"A brother."

"What's his name?"

"Matt."

Slowly, Marritt reached into his pocket and drew out a page of notes. "Does he by any chance live at three-ten East Sixty-ninth Street?"

"How . . . what made you ask that?"

"Just answer my question. Is that his correct address?"

"Yes."

"What was his connection with Doug Nicholas?"

Slowly, Rubes gathered his breath. "I'm afraid you'll have to ask him that."

"Mr. Reuben. Don't play games with me. What was your brother's connection with Doug Nicholas?"

"I'm sorry. I just don't know the answer."

"Were you sending customers to Doug Nicholas?"

"No."

"What about your girlfriend?"

"She wasn't either."

"Then it's a little strange, isn't it, that your brother's name should wind up in a dead man's address book?"

Confused, Rubes nodded.

"So answer me, Mr. Reuben. Do you—" Marritt stopped in mid-sentence, then stood up and reached for his coat. "Forget it," he said. "I have no further questions. On a personal level, you seem like a nice enough young fellow. Investigatively speaking, you're worthless."

"Investigatively worthless." The phrase hung in the air after Marritt had left. Shaking his head, Rubes walked downstairs to the street. It was chillier outside than expected, and he hunched his shoulders protectively against the wind. Shuffling his feet through curled brown leaves on the sidewalk, he trod slowly up Riverside Drive, oblivious to the finely etched full moon above.

Why had Marritt asked about Matt? Rubes ran the question through his mind. Had he ever told Matt that Doug was a dealer? Yes, months ago, when he and Aggy remet . . . Had Matt made a buy? Maybe, but he hadn't told Rubes about it . . . Why was Matt's name in Doug's book? Maybe they were friends; but Matt hadn't mentioned that either. It didn't make sense; unless, of course . . .

Enough! Rubes kicked at a tin can and listened as it clattered into the gutter. At 79th Street, he stopped and contemplated which way to turn. If he walked toward the museum, he might run into Aggy on her way home.

The wind was cold. Aggy liked winter. Rubes didn't, and its proximity depressed him. It was a bleak, lonely time of year and, all too often, an unhappy one. Christmas and the presents he never had enough money to buy; too many holidays spent alone. Always a feeling of loneliness. That was the worst part—the loneliness. There was never anyone to share himself with. Sooner or later, every winter memory turned into a bad one.

The vase—dark, deep blue china with tiny flowers etched into its side. When Rubes was nine, he had wanted desperately to give it to his parents for Christmas. For weeks, he had seen it in the gift-shop window, surrounded by tinsel and boughs of pine—the prettiest vase ever. Except the vase cost four dollars and ninety-five cents, and Rubes only had three dollars.

Matt kept his money in a small tin box in the back of his bureau drawer. Three days before Christmas, Rubes snuck into Matt's room and took two dollars—four quarters and a dollar bill. That evening, when the blue china vase with flowers was safely gift-wrapped in Rubes's closet, Matt noticed that two dollars was missing.

"Did you take it?" he demanded of Rubes.

"No."

Matt looked at his little brother. "How much money do you have in your room?"

"Nothing."

"How come?"

"I spent it all on Mommy and Daddy's present."

"How much did you spend?"

"Five dollars."

"Where did you get it?"

Rubes's lower lip began to tremble.

"Where did you get it?"

He started to cry.

Matt looked down at his brother and took a step back. "Maybe I made a mistake," he said. "I thought I was missing four quarters and a dollar bill. Maybe I was wrong."

The day after Christmas, Rubes took two dollars from his Christmas money and put it inside the tin box in Matt's drawer. Matt never said a word about the incident again—not to Rubes, not to their parents.

A few days later, Rubes's mother broke the vase while dusting and threw the pieces in the garbage. By the time father came home from work, the garbage had been carted away. It was too late to glue the vase back together again.

"Would you like a second dessert?" Matt asked.

"No thanks, I'm full." Aggy reached into her purse and took out two dollars. "This is for my share."

"I'll be glad to treat."

"That's all right," she answered. "I'm used to paying for myself."

They walked outside the restaurant and stopped at the curb.

"I'll walk you home," Matt offered.

"No need. The streets around here are pretty safe." She looked at him and smiled. "Thank you. It wasn't a bad night. You're not all mean after all."

"Only ninety percent?"

"Eighty-five. I'll see you in class next Wednesday night. In fact, come to think of it, I'll see you at Princeton this Saturday."

Matt hailed a taxi and was gone. Aggy turned toward West End Avenue. On the corner of Broadway and 79th Street, she ran into Rubes, who walked her the rest of the way home.

CHAPTER 12

"Is that The Blonde?" Aggy queried with capital-letter inflection in her voice.

"I guess so," Rubes answered.

They were standing on the curb in front of Aggy's apartment, waiting for an approaching blue sedan with Matt in the driver's seat and an unidentified object at his side.

Aggy was less than enthusiastic about the day ahead. She didn't like football and had no desire to partake in the inevitable competition between Rubes and Matt as to who had the more desirable date. Also, at times, the unspoken tensions between the brothers left her anxious and uncomfortable. Still, the day had come, and like it or not she was going to Princeton. For Rubes's sake, she'd pull herself together for the show. She owed him that much—why, she wasn't sure.

"Hello again," Matt said as Aggy climbed into the back seat. The "again," she knew, was a double entendre. As far as Rubes was concerned, it referred to the dinner they had shared as a trio at her apartment the week before. She wouldn't mention the museum unless Matt brought it up first.

"Hello back," Aggy answered.

The Blonde was introduced, and the blue sedan drew away from the curb heading downtown toward the Lincoln Tunnel. Matt's companion had a striking body, accentuated by long blonde hair that hung down in ringlets to her bulging breasts. But I'm brighter, Aggy told herself. And, as if to prove it, as the car wound its way down the West Side Highway, she began to discourse in animated fashion on everything from American history ("Did you know the Pony Express was only a year old when it was made obsolete by the telegraph?") to her own peculiar view of science ("The four elements in nature should more properly be viewed as five—earth, air, fire, water and hot fudge sauce").

The Blonde lit number one in what would become a chain of cigarettes.

Rubes stared out the window, wondering about his confrontation several days earlier with Marritt.

"How come you're so quiet?" he heard Aggy ask. "You haven't said a word since we started."

"You have to be silently philosophical about Columbia football," Rubes answered.

Matt steered the car through the Lincoln Tunnel and onto the New Jersey Turnpike. "This is Matthew Reuben, speaking of sports," he intoned in a mock nasal voice, "and I'm talking with one of the great fans in Columbia University's hapless football history. Rubes, could you tell us what to expect from today's ballgame?"

"Well, Matthew," Rubes answered, snapping back to the present. "I look for a hard-fought game, with the Columbia Lions coming out on top."

"The eternal optimist, if ever there was one," Matt countered, going for the jugular. "But the analysis, sports fans, is flawed. This year's edition of the Columbia Lions has an offense that can't move the ball against a stiff wind. The quarterback is far more adept at spotting the opposing middle linebacker than his own receivers and, in truth, has to pitch out to his fullback whenever Columbia wants to throw a long pass."

The wail of a police siren interrupted the monologue. Pulling to the side of the road, Matt stopped the car and waited. A New Jersey State Trooper pulled up behind and ambled over. Matt rolled down the window.

"Yes, sir?"

"What's the speed limit on this highway, son?"

"I thought it was fifty-five."

"It is. You've been doing seventy for two miles. I've been clocking you."

"I'm sorry."

"Give me your license and registration."

(Handing them over) "Couldn't . . ."

"Now be quiet while I write this out."

(For form's sake) "But . . ."

"I said be quiet."

The Blonde took out a compact and began redistributing the blue eye shadow around her eyelids. "Is the makeup too much?" she asked, addressing the question to no one in particular.

"Not really," Aggy thought. "People will just think you're a lower-class file clerk from the Bronx."

The cop leaned through the window and handed the ticket to Matt.

"Very good," Rubes said when they began driving again. "Twenty-five miles and one ticket. At that rate, you'll get five speeding tickets this afternoon."

"Shut up," Matt snapped.

"This is Matthew Reuben, speaking of sports," Rubes mimicked, "and I'm talking with internationally famous racing driver A. J. Foyt. A. J.—"

"Shut up, I said. Jesus, you can be such a baby."

Matt covered the next ten miles with considerably more caution and shifted onto Route 1, where they stopped for gas. Rubes went inside to check the vending machines. The sandwich machine had a big "OUT OF ORDER" sign across its face. The candy machine had a strip of adhesive over the coin slot. An hour later, they arrived at Palmer Stadium in Princeton. "I have to go to the bathroom," The Blonde announced.

"Go ahead," Matt told her. "We'll get the tickets."

Aggy accompanied The Blonde to the ladies' room. Rubes followed Matt. Princeton being the home team, Matt pointed out at the ticket window, it was only logical that they sit on the Princeton side. Actually, they sat on the Princeton side when the game was at Columbia too, but that was irrelevant. Together, they bought the tickets and waited for the women to return.

"I want to ask you something," Rubes said.

"Go ahead."

"Three nights ago, I had a visit from a cop named Marritt."

Matt waited. "What's the question?" he asked at last.

"What was your connection with Doug Nicholas?"

"Yoohoo," The Blonde interrupted. "We're back."

The game was anticlimactic. Princeton won. They always did. Twenty thousand spectators spent most of the afternoon watching Princeton tacklers in orange-and-black uniforms swarm over the Columbia quarterback while Princeton running backs tore gaping holes in the Columbia line. The highlight of the day was watching Princeton's two-hundred-seventy-pound All-Ivy, All-American tackle—Goliath Richardson III—in action. "Golly," as he was known to his adoring fans, was the third in a line of blue-blooded Princetonians stretching back to Goliath

Richardson I, who had led a successful student uprising against the efforts of University President Woodrow Wilson to abolish eating clubs at Princeton in 1909. Having been soundly trounced by Goliath I, Wilson left Princeton to assume the Governorship of New Jersey and, later, the Presidency of the United States. Goliath Richardson I proceeded to make a fortune in industry and sire two-hundred-seventy-pound, blond-haired, blue-eyed offensive tackles.

The postgame ride back to New York was quieter than the one out. Only The Blonde was talking, and she wasn't very bright. "Who's Walter Mondale?" she asked when Aggy, hoping to shut her up, steered the conversation to politics.

Matt winced.

"A former Vice-President of the United States," Aggy informed her.

"I don't see how that's relevant," The Blonde opined. "Besides, politics bore me."

"I never would have guessed," Aggy challenged. "Should we talk about lipstick?"

"Very clever," Matt countered, riding gallantly to The Blonde's rescue. "Maybe you should enter the Miss Subways contest."

"*Ms.* Subways to you," Aggy answered.

"You're very ill-mannered," huffed The Blonde. "I think you're just jealous because I'm with Matt."

"Maybe," Aggy told herself. "But you're about to pay for saying it."

"Hey sweetheart," she countered. "Do me a favor. Go wrap your legs around a bathtub faucet and let it pour."

Rubes missed it all. He was fixating on Doug Nicholas.

CHAPTER 13

How much did Marritt know? Why had he asked about Matt?

Rubes sat on the bed in Aggy's apartment and leaned against the headboard. Aggy was sitting up straight, gesturing with both arms.

"Okay," she said. "I'm willing to admit that my behavior on the way back from Princeton this afternoon wasn't exactly perfect. But really, that blonde is the dumbest thing I've ever seen. I think she has Pinocchio Syndrome. Every time she says something stupid, her breasts seem to grow another quarter of an inch. The only excuse I can think of for Matt's dating her is that he got desperate because he was behind for the month in filling his sexual quota."

"It's not Matt's fault she has large breasts."

"No, it's not Matt's fault she has large breasts, and it's not Matt's fault she's stupid. But he is the one who goes out with her."

Should he tell her that Marritt had asked about Matt? Probably not. What was it their father had told them once during one of their interminable sibling squabbles? "You're brothers. Don't forget that, ever. Friends come and go. You'll be brothers forever." He couldn't trust Aggy the way he could trust Matt.

"Congratulations," Aggy was saying. "You won."

"Huh?"

"You won. Isn't that what this afternoon was all

about? I beat up on The Blonde. So now you've got your great victory, and you can go back to being stepped on until next year when, God willing, Matt will be in another slump and you'll win the Columbia-Princeton-Desirable-Date Competition all over again."

"What are you talking about?"

"Come off it, Reuben. I saw it here at dinner last Friday night, and I saw it again today at Princeton. He runs you. It's the most patronizing thing I've ever seen. You talk; he interrupts. He leads; you follow. And every now and then, to show you're not totally out of it, you shove me forward and shout, 'Look! I've got Aggy.' What is it with you and Matt?"

Rubes sat silent.

"Be honest. What do you really think of your brother?"

"I don't know," Rubes said, running a finger along the edge of the bed. "When I was little, I used to think maybe I'd been adopted—that Matt was my parent's natural child and I wasn't. He always did everything better. He was better in sports; he was better in school; he was better with girls; he was everything I wasn't. On the subway one day last week, I was standing next to a good-looking woman. The subway jerked and I jostled against her. I couldn't help it. Then my arm brushed against her side and she pulled away. If it had been Matt, she would have pulled closer."

Aggy stared. "Is that what you're all about? Is that what makes Matt so wonderful—he leans against women on the subway?" Her anger was growing. "Don't you understand how hollow your brother is? He has no insides. All he wants out of life is self-gratification while you stand on the sidelines and cheer."

"Don't talk that way."

"Why not?"

"Because it's not nice."

Aggy's hands shot into the air. "I really don't care."

"Why is it so hard for you to accept the fact that I love my brother?"

"Because he doesn't love you . . . I'm sorry. I shouldn't have said that."

Rubes shook his head. "He used to love me. And he meant a lot to me. He was someone I used to look up to, someone I was proud of."

"But you don't love someone for what they were. You care about them for what they are *now,* or else you've stopped loving them. Don't you understand that?"

"Then I love him for what he is . . . And I love you."

There it was!

"Oh, Christ! I don't need this." Wearily, Aggy sagged against the headboard. "You haven't grown up at all in five years. And to be honest, I don't think you have any idea what love is."

"Do you?"

"I know what it isn't. And I don't like the pedestal you've put me on. Sometimes I think I'm the new Matt. Everything I do is right. Nothing I do is wrong. All I am is an extension of yourself, someone you're using to create an idyllic self-image and fulfill some sort of dream. Well, I'm tired of being what other people want me to be, and I'm not what you think I am. You don't have the foggiest idea what goes on inside my head. I don't think you even care whether or not you make me happy—only whether you make me happy enough to stay with you."

Why did she feel so guilty when she yelled at

him? Somewhere inside, a scene was playing—Aggy on her deathbed, fifty years in the future, with Rubes grieving at her side. "Goddamn it!" she wanted to scream. "Do I even have to feel guilty about dying?"

"I'm sorry," she said. "I don't mean to upset you, but you aren't the only one with problems. I have problems too . . ."

It was just past eleven and she was tired. Rubes was so pathetic she didn't have the heart to send him home . . . "Let's go to sleep," she said.

"Can't we talk about it," he pleaded.

"In the morning. I'm tired and I got my period this afternoon. Go to sleep."

They undressed without touching and crawled beneath the covers on separate sides of the bed. That done, they lay in the darkness.

It was going wrong. Rubes knew it. Everything was crumbling. All the bad memories were coming back to haunt him. The child playing Monopoly alone because his only friends were imaginary ones . . . Listening to ballgames on the radio late at night because he desperately wanted a live voice to talk with him . . . Waiting for the mailman when there was never any mail . . . Looking forward to a special date, picking her up, and hearing the first words out of her mouth—"I don't feel well. We'll have to make it an early evening." . . . When he was little, he had stuttered. . . .

Didn't Aggy realize how he felt about her? Wasn't that enough? The murder had upset her. That was it. The murder and the abortion and the dreams. No wonder she was upset. If his next-door neighbor had been murdered, he wouldn't be so chipper either. Wasn't that what Matt had said on Columbus Day? "Your next-door neighbor wasn't murdered; it was Aggy's." Something like that. . . . It wasn't Matt's fault that mother and father had loved him more than Rubes. When the two of them were kids and mother served chocolate sundaes for dessert, she had always given more fudge sauce to Matt. . . . What to do about Matt?

Aggy lay on her back and stared at the shadow of leaves across the ceiling. Life wasn't supposed to be like this.

The leaves etched a picture in her mind. A chapel in the snow . . . A wedding . . . Separate footprints leading into the church . . . Footprints united as the bride and groom left together in the snow.

The chapel vanished and she saw elves. She'd forgotten about them. When she was a child, two huge maple trees had framed her bedroom window. When they swayed in the nighttime breeze, the pattern of leaves against the moonlight played on the wall above her bed. . . . Elves . . . Gnomes . . . Vicious evil creatures frolicking in the night . . . Terrifying shadows playing above her. Until age eight, Aggy went to sleep with her hands over her eyes to fend off the onslaught.

Rubes's voice interrupted her thoughts.

"Do you remember when you stopped seeing me . . . the last time, when we were in college?"

"I suppose so," she said.

"I wanted to see you so badly. I used to hang around the places you might be so I could catch a glimpse of you. Once I saw you through the window of the university bookstore and went inside so I could walk you home. You were wearing a red sweater. Do you remember?"

"Why are you telling me this?"

"I don't know. I guess I just want you to know. Do you remember?"

"No."

"Oh."

Aggy closed her eyes.

"Would it be all right if I put my hand on your breast?"

"Pleast don't."

All around, she was surrounded by people who were unhappy. Rubes . . . Matt . . . Doug had seemed unhappy too. She didn't want to be like them. She wanted birch trees and homemade ice cream and reading late at night with someone she loved. Someone strong. Men found her desirable. She knew that. She could hold her own physically, intellectually and every other way with the best of them. So why was she sharing her bed with Rubes?

"At least he's safe," Aggy told herself as she drifted toward sleep. "At least Rubes is safe . . ."

And then something flashed through her mind, so terrifying that she pushed it away without ever acknowledging its presence, so fast that she saw only the gleam of its heel as it fled.

CHAPTER 14

Matt lay on his bed without any clothes on. The Blonde was huge. Propped on her elbow, she smiled and turned her shoulders toward him. As she did, her breasts swung across her body and suspended momentarily in midair before crashing to her chest.

He had just had her, and he didn't want her anymore. She had bad stretch marks, and her breasts sagged more than was right. They had no form and he wished she weren't there. He couldn't stand it when she touched his face.

"Do you want me to spend the night?" she asked.

Matt stared at the mirror by the bed. "Not really."

She recoiled at his frankness. "You want the fuck-and-run special. Is that it?"

"I'm sorry," he answered. "I didn't mean it that way. You can stay if you want."

"That's all right," she said, icy hurt. "I'm leaving. Could I please have cab fare?"

Matt handed her a five-dollar bill. She dressed and was gone.

"Shit," he said to himself, slumping on the sofa. "What's wrong with me?"

Maybe it was the game that had thrown him—seeing Rubes with Aggy. That plus the question: "What was your connection with Doug Nicholas?" Leave it to Rubes to make any set of circumstances difficult.

He was glad The Blonde had gone. Her breath smelled of coffee and cigarettes. She was the type of broad who'd leave a bra hanging in the bathroom so, when you went to take a leak, you'd see on the label that she was a double-D. Of course, he was the type who would look.

Aggy and The Blonde. What a match-up. In this corner, ladies and gentlemen, wearing red trunks, five feet seven inches tall, one hundred and twenty-three pounds, 34-24-34 . . . Agatha Tilden.

And in this corner, wearing gold trunks with white trim, five feet seven inches, one hundred and thirty-five pounds, 38-27-37 . . . The Titanic-Breasted Blonde . . .

The roar of the crowd swelled as the referee gave both fighters their instructions. Then they returned to their respective corners, awaiting the start of round one.

At the bell, Aggy came out and jabbed tentatively with her left hand . . . once . . . twice . . . three times. Sensing her opponent's anxiety, The Blonde plowed forward with a heavy two-fisted attack to the body that sent Aggy reeling backwards. The Blonde bored in, pummeling Aggy to the rib cage with vicious lefts and rights, battering her chest with solid blows. Desperately, Aggy tried to ward her off, but to no avail. Power oozed from The Blonde's fists, and she pushed forward with each assault as the crowd grew more and more excited.

Out of nowhere, Aggy threw a right uppercut landing solidly on The Blonde's chin. Slipping away from the ropes as her adversary's knees wobbled, Aggy began to pepper her heavier opponent with cobralike jabs. The Blonde was tiring. A hard right sent her backwards, and Aggy followed it up with a left hook that dug beneath The Blonde's right breast. A left-right combination to the midsection doubled her over, and Aggy began measuring The Blonde for another right. Jab . . . jab . . . A thunderous right hand crashed against The Blonde's jaw, toppling her to the canvas.

One . . . two . . . three . . . As the referee started his count, The Blonde raised herself on one elbow and gazed through glassy eyes toward the delirious crowd . . . Four . . . five . . . six . . . seven . . . eight . . . She wasn't going to make it . . . Nine . . . ten . . . "It's all over," the announcer shrieked. "It's all over. . . . The time, two minutes and ten seconds of the first round. . . . The winner by a knockout, Agatha Tilden."

The crowd surged forward, watching Aggy's every move, cheering as her sleek gleaming body glistened under the hot ring lights, beads of moisture dripping from her long black hair. And somewhere, off to the side, Rubes was cheering. . . . And Matt was alone . . . lying naked on the bed in his apartment.

"Fuck that," Matt said aloud, lifting himself from the bed and walking to the bathroom. Glancing at his reflection in the mirror, he turned the shower on very hot, then stepped inside. For longer than usual, he stood beneath the spray, letting the water pour over him at full pressure, feeling his skin come alive. Only when the bathroom was completely fogged did he lessen the steam, turning the water cold and letting it pour down while his heart pounded. By the time he toweled himself dry, The Blonde was out of his thoughts, having been replaced by a stream of consciousness gushing forth the past.

Rubes was a funny kid to have as a younger brother. He never quite got the hang of things. Matt remembered the time, maybe fifteen years earlier, when Rubes, sitting cross-legged on the floor, had watched in fascination as his older brother lit a candle and passed an index finger through the flame.

"See," Matt said, holding his finger up with a grin. "It doesn't hurt. Want to try?"

"No."

"Come on. I'll show you how."

Rubes shrank back from the candle. "I don't want to."

"Come on," Matt urged, grabbing hold of his brother's hand and forcing it toward the flame. "Don't be a baby."

"I'm not a baby."

"Then let me show you how."

Rubes pulled his hand away. "I'll do it myself."

"But you don't know how."

"I'll do it myself."

Hand trembling, Rubes extended a finger and pushed it toward the flame. The fire was hot and he wanted to pull away, but Matt was watching. Slowly, he pushed closer; then, eyes closed, he shoved the finger forward. A low hiss punctured the air and Rubes drew back, holding his scorched finger in pain.

"You passed it through too high." Matt grinned. "If you'd let me show you how, you wouldn't have burned yourself."

Shortly after that, Matt remembered, a robin had made its nest in a tree by the front porch of their home. One day in late spring, father brought a ladder from the basement and set it against the tree. Taking turns, the brothers climbed to the top and peered down. There, nestled inside the nest, was an egg—perfectly shaped; a light, bright, beautiful blue.

"Don't touch it," father warned. "You can bring the ladder out to look at it whenever you want, but don't touch."

The egg never hatched. Instead, for whatever reason, it turned rotten. One night, late that summer, Rubes crept into Matt's room. "I touched it," he said.

"What?"

"I touched it . . . the egg."

"What egg?"

"In the nest on the tree by the front porch. I climbed the ladder to look every day and, one afternoon, I touched it." Rubes started to cry. "I killed it. I killed the baby robin."

"It's funny," Matt thought to himself, returning to present-day reality. Rubes cried all the time as a kid; Matt hardly at all, not even when their father died. Rubes had taken the death much harder. Then, two weeks after the funeral, mother announced they were taking in Mrs. Graff, a boarder who would sleep in Rubes's room. What a scene that had been. "Why can't she take Matt's room? He's away at Princeton."

"She doesn't want to walk up stairs," mother answered.

"Okay. Then I'll sleep in Matt's room."

"No, you won't. That's his room as long as he wants it."

"She's gone bananas," Rubes told Matt that night as they talked long-distance on the telephone. "She put Mrs. Graff in my room and won't let me take yours. She told me to sleep in the living room and store my things in the attic."

Not even Matt could argue the logic of that. "Look, tell her I don't want my room anymore. It's yours."

"No it's not," mother responded that night. "You sleep in the living room." A month later, she told Rubes he was old enough to be out on his own. Rubes was seventeen years old. For the first time in his life, he flew off the handle.

"It's my house as much as yours," he raged. "My father left it for me. Not for fucking Mrs. Graff. For me."

"If I were you," mother answered, "I wouldn't stay where I wasn't wanted." Then she picked up the telephone and called the police. Rubes was sitting on the front porch, tears streaming down his face, when two cops arrived. Neither cop wrote anything down as mother spoke.

"He don't look too violent to me, lady," the police sergeant said.

"It's okay," Rubes told them. "I'm leaving. Give me a couple of hours to get my things together and I'll be gone. I don't want to cause any trouble."

"Sure," the sergeant said. "Take as much time as you need. We won't be back."

Rubes was gone a few hours later. He spent the rest of the school year with the family of a friend and, the following fall, enrolled in college. He never saw mother again. Matt saw her as seldom as possible. On those few occasions when there was a need for family, Rubes and Matt relied on each other.

Of course, Matt could rely on himself and that was a big plus. When no one else was there, he could go it alone. He didn't mind it, except for an occasional holiday. Last Christmas had been bad. Usually he and Rubes spent Christmas together. This time, though, Rubes had gone south and Matt played his invitations poorly. Actually, there hadn't been too many to play. One from a woman he didn't want to be with and another which could have meant traveling to Boston. That was how Matt came to spend Christmas alone. Maybe the holidays were a time to reap what was sown. It didn't really matter.

The coffee shop had been nearly empty when Matt walked in a little after noon. A small piece of mistletoe hung above the doorway. Red and white candy canes dotted the walls. The man behind the cash register had the radio on and the sound of carols permeated the air.

"I suppose I should have turkey," Matt thought to himself. "I like brisket of beef better, but it's Christmas." His eyes scanned the menu. The turkey came with French fries and a vegetable. All white meat was eighty cents extra. "It's Christmas; why not splurge?" he said to himself.

The menu had splotches of gravy strewn across it. The radio by the cash register was too loud.

Hark the Herald Angels sing
Glory to the newborn King
Peace on earth and mercy mild
God and sinners reconciled . . .

"A piece of chocolate cake too," he instructed the waitress. "You can bring it all together if you want."

Joyful all ye nations rise
Join the triumph of the skies
With angelic hosts proclaim
Christ is born in Bethlehem . . .

The music bugged him. Christmas carols had always made him sad. They were a reminder that a piece of his life was missing.

Pleased as man with man doth dwell
Jesus our Emmanuel
Hark the Herald Angels sing
Glory to the newborn King.

There was too much gristle in the turkey. Matt

ate as much as he could and left the rest, pushing the plate away as he stood up from the table.

"Merry Christmas," the cashier intoned as Matt paid the check and stuffed his change in a back pocket.

"You too," he answered, passing through the door, buttoning up his coat against the chill December air.

CHAPTER 15

Aggy drifted into a fitful sleep with Rubes at her side, and the wind began to swirl. She pulled the covers up around her neck, and it blew harder, kicking up dirt and spitting drops of blood against her hair. Across the hall, the storm raged even louder, buffeting faceless forms against the wall. Lightning flashed and thunder exploded in the night.

Her hair had turned to willow reeds, cutting her face, whipping in the storm. A man in a doctor's white coat stood beside her, with tongs attached to his elbows where his forearms should have been. She tried to see his face, but her eyes couldn't reach above the tongs. Desperately, she grabbed for a knife and began hacking at the reeds. "It sparkles," the doctor said.

The door blew open and a clown bounded into the room. Aggy sat upright. The clown, bathed in blood, stared. A broad grin crossed its face, and it pointed with a bloodstained dagger. The door closed and the clown grew dim. Its body faded; the head began to glow. Laughter filled the room. The crazed eyes came closer. Aggy screamed and the apparition vanished.

Rubes held her as she cried. She was more afraid than before, and her body shook violently. "I heard it," she sobbed. "I heard it when Doug was murdered."

"What did you hear?"

"The dream."

"What dream?"

She kept crying.

"Start with tonight," he pleaded. "What do you remember about tonight?"

"The clown."

"What clown?"

She shuddered . . . "The eyes . . . the mouth . . ."

"Go on."

"The grin . . ." She began to cry again.

Rubes's throat tightened and his eyes closed. "She knows," he thought to himself. "Somewhere inside, she knows."

CHAPTER 16

The jangling of the telephone woke Aggy on Sunday morning. Reaching across Rubes, she picked up the receiver, then shook him gently.

"It's for you."

"Huh?"

"It's Matt."

Rubes took the phone and grunted to the wide-awake voice on the other end of the line.

"I tried to get you at home," Matt said, "but there wasn't any answer, so I figured you were with Aggy."

"How did you get the number?"

"It's in the phone book. Listen. Do you want to go on a picnic?"

Rubes pondered the proposition. "Why?"

"Because it's nice out, and we should spend some time together."

"We were together yesterday at Princeton."

"That wasn't alone," came the reply. "Look, I'll bring the food and pick you up at your place around noon. What do you say?"

"Let me think about it."

"See you at noon." (Click)

Rubes put down the receiver and turned to Aggy. "I'm going on a picnic."

She barely opened her eyes. "It sounded to me like he hung up on you."

"He did, but only after I was invited."

"He didn't invite you, he ordered you. Fuck him."

"I think I'll go. I want to talk to him about your latest dream."

Aggy shrugged. "So go, already. I can't stop you."

As promised, Matt was on Rubes's doorstep at noon. "I got the stuff at the delicatessen on Broadway you're always talking about," he announced, holding up a large shopping bag filled with parcels.

"What did you bring?"

"Bagels, lox, two kinds of cheese, and chicken salad. Plus a bottle of wine. All we need is an old blanket."

Rubes leaned over his bed and removed the top cover. "It needs cleaning anyway," he explained. "This way I won't be able to avoid taking it to the laundry."

Matt made a face. "That's one way of looking at it. Come on, let's go."

They walked downstairs, then toward Broadway. "Aggy had a dream last night," Rubes said as they neared the park. "She's had them every night this week."

Matt was a study of indifference. "What about?" he asked at last.

"The murder."

There was no response.

"The dreams are bloody and very frightening. At first, there were just sounds. Then there were images. Last night she saw who killed Doug Nicholas."

Matt's head turned slightly. "Who was it?"

"She doesn't know yet. The murderer was dressed in a clown suit . . . in the dream, that is. He came into Aggy's room with a dagger dripping with blood and vanished when she screamed. The clown was wearing a blue suit. That's the same color shirt you wore yesterday to Princeton."

Matt stopped and turned to face Rubes directly. "Are you suggesting that I dressed up like a clown, snuck into Aggy's apartment last night, cavorted around the room with a blood-soaked dagger, and disappeared into thin air when she woke up?"

Rubes was momentarily flustered. "Dreams tell a lot about what goes on in someone's subconscious," he said at last.

Matt shook his head. "Then maybe it was you—or have you forgotten, you wore blue jeans to the game yesterday."

Oblivious to the stream of passersby, they entered the park.

"Look!" Matt said, picking up the conversation. "Let's level with each other. What's this nonsense all about?"

Rubes didn't answer.

"Come on! Yesterday, you hit me with a question about my connection with Doug Nicholas. Today you start making cryptic comments about a dream your girlfriend had. What's going on?"

Over twenty years of suppressed bitterness poured forth with Rubes's words: "I've watched you. I've seen it now for over a week. I saw your face the night Aggy started to remember. You did it. *You killed Doug Nicholas.*"

Matt stared incredulously. "You're a flaming idiot."

"Don't say that."

"You're stark raving mad."

"No I'm not. I told you about Doug Nicholas right after I met Aggy. You said you needed grass, and I told you where you could get some. You knew he was a dealer."

"So what!"

"And you bought from him. Marritt said your name was in his address book."

"That doesn't mean anything."

"And when you read the *New York Times* on Columbus Day, you remembered that Aggy lived at three sixty-six West End Avenue. How did you remember the exact address?"

Matt said nothing.

"Do you always read the police blotter in the *New York Times*? Or just when you're looking for something in particular?"

"You're crazy."

"And the police! Why didn't you want me to call the police when Aggy started to cry? . . . I shouldn't call the police but, for days before that, you were full of questions about helping the police. 'Did Aggy hear anything, Rubes? . . . What does she remember, Rubes? . . . Could she help the police, Rubes?' . . . And your time—your precious valuable time. You've always been too busy to give me more than a few hours a month but, ever since they found Doug's body, you've been living on my doorstep."

Matt kept his temper, barely. "I haven't been living on your doorstep. I saw you for brunch two weeks ago, dinner last Friday, and the football game yesterday. And now today. That's four times in two weeks. Once for our regular brunch, once to meet your girlfriend, and once for the football game we go to every year. I called today—look, I'll be honest. I called today because I'm lonely. Last night was a bad night. So I called this morning, and now I get this shit. For the first time in your life, you have a girlfriend, and it's making you nuttier than she is."

"Where were you?" Rubes pressed. "The night Doug Nicholas was killed, where were you?"

"How do I know?" Matt snapped. "I don't even know when he was killed, and neither does Aggy. Did you ask her? Does she know when he was killed? No!

All she knows is that she thinks she heard it. Where were you the night he was killed? You don't know either, do you? Maybe *you* did it. After all, what better way to cover up for yourself than by making wild accusations."

Rubes weakened and, as he did, Matt picked up strength. "You don't know where you were; but we can assume you weren't in bed with Aggy because, if you had been, you would have heard it too, wouldn't you? You would have called the police and made sure everything was all right. . . . Or don't you go to bed with her?"

Rubes said nothing.

"I suppose you do. She's been around long enough. Since age seventeen, I think she said."

"That's enough."

"Jesus! You two have the most infantile relationship I've ever seen. You look at her like an eight-year-old looks at Mary Tyler Moore."

"Stop it."

"Does she make you wear cutoff jeans to bed?"

"Stop it!" Rubes shouted.

Matt gritted his teeth. Then, suddenly, his voice dropped. "Look, Rubes. I'm sorry. This isn't what I wanted. I didn't call this morning to fight. I was looking forward to today as simple straightforward time together. We're brothers, but sometimes I feel like a stranger to you. And there are too many times I feel alone. Last Friday, when you were talking about your vision of heaven—the room where you could stay for an eternity—I asked myself afterward, who was the special person I'd want to see again after I died? I couldn't think of anyone. That's when I decided I should reach out to people. I thought about it some more last night. I'm reaching out to you. Don't you understand?"

There was no answer.

"Look," Matt pressed. "I apologize for some of the things I just said. I didn't mean them, but you were making some pretty heavy accusations. You know that, don't you?"

Rubes nodded.

"And I'd just as soon you keep them to yourself. There are enough things in Aggy's head right now without your adding my name to the list." Reaching out, Matt took Rubes by the shoulders with both hands. "I'm your brother. We came out of the same womb. I didn't kill Doug Nicholas."

"I want to believe you."

"You have to believe me. Friends come and go. We'll always be brothers. Remember that. When the chips are down, I'm all you've got."

Rubes felt an uneasy sensation, as though Matt was about to read his mind.

"She's not the dream you're searching for who will turn your life around." Matt said it gently, incontrovertibly. "Don't you understand? Aggy doesn't love you."

"Do you?"

"Yes."

"Then say it."

Matt turned his head in confusion. "Say what?"

"That you love me . . . Say it, out loud."

"That's silly."

"Say it," Rubes ordered.

"I love you."

They walked to the center of Central Park, where a large crowd had gathered in a noisy circle. Craning his neck, Rubes peered over the front row and saw two pairs of combatants squared off in a game of "chicken." On one side, a short, bull-shouldered

Puerto Rican had lifted a Latin girl onto his shoulders and was pawing the dirt with his foot waiting for combat. Across the ring, a taller, long-haired adversary struggled to lift a buxom girl into position on his shoulders. On signal, the two pairs charged one another and collided, the "horsemen" trying to maintain balance while their "riders" flailed away, attempting to topple one another. The crowd roared with approval, letting loose with cries of "Mira, mira, amigo" when the Latin girl ripped open her opponent's blouse, revealing fleshy breasts sagging over the top of a graying bra.

Rubes and Matt watched two falls, then wandered off. "What a bunch," Matt observed. "They're so dull, I'd like to rub their heads together. Maybe the friction between the blocks of wood would fire a spark of imagination."

Rubes ignored the comment and looked up toward the sky. An ominous blanket of angry gray clouds had begun to gather.

"And after that," Matt continued, "I'd like to go down to Puerto Rico and wander through the streets of San Juan with a portable cassette recorder blaring Beethoven."

The first drops of rain fell. . . . A trio of roller-skaters wheeled by. . . . Then the clouds opened and the downpour began.

"I still want to picnic," Matt shouted as he and Rubes ran for cover.

"We'll get soaked."

"Not on the carousel. It has a canopy."

"You're crazy," Rubes yelled from five yards behind.

They ran through the rain for about a hundred yards—Matt in the lead with the picnic bag under his arm, Rubes close on his shoulder. At the south end of the park, panting and out of breath, they came to the carousel, its organ sounding cheerfully above the storm.

"Ten tickets, please," Matt said, handing the woman at the change booth a five-dollar bill. "This is for five rides each," he said as he gave the tickets to the attendant.

Passing the single horses, Rubes and Matt mounted one of four large wooden carousel chariots and spread the picnic blanket on the chariot floor. As the rain beat down on the canopy above, the organ played louder and the carousel began to turn.

"Please pass the chicken salad."

"I'll trade you for a bagel."

A picnic on the carousel! When all was said and done, Matt was a genius. Rubes had no choice but to look up to him. Anyone who had ever been a little brother could understand.

CHAPTER 17

To Lieutenant Richard Marritt
in grateful appreciation for his work with us,
the boys of the Police Athletic League.

"Not bad, is it?" Marritt asked rhetorically, stepping back from the wall and viewing his latest acquisition with satisfaction.

"It's a little crooked," Dema volunteered. "Raise it a bit on the right."

"Done," said the detective, adjusting the plaque. "It's nice to know you're appreciated." Moving behind his desk, Marritt settled in the chair and grinned. "You know something, Dema. Being a good cop is probably the most idealistic job in the world. Don't ever forget that. And I'll tell you something else. There's no such thing as a bad kid. They're all good until someone ruins them."

The detective leaned back, hands clasped behind his head. "Wait till you're a parent. You'll see. You'll bitch and you'll scream, give the kids hell. One day, you're afraid you're spoiling them, the next day you think you're too tough. Then Father's Day comes around, they give you that present with the sweet little look in their eyes, and bingo, it's all worthwhile. If you're really lucky, one of them will ask, If there's a Father's Day and a Mother's Day, how come there isn't a Children's Day?'" Marritt's eyes twinkled with laughter. "That's when you tell them, 'Every day is Children's Day.'" He threw his hands in the air and laughed aloud.

"So much for pleasantries," he said when his mirth had subsided. "What do we have that's new on Doug Nicholas?"

"Not much," Dema answered. "I checked with the telephone company, but all that turned up were a couple of long-distance calls each month to Texas. I checked the number. It's a pusher who's already under surveillance by the FBI, but he doesn't tie into this. All he does is sell, and the Bureau says he hasn't left Texas for almost a year.

"Why don't they arrest him?"

"They're hoping he'll lead them on to someone bigger."

"Bright thinking. What else?"

"I've been making the rounds of Doug Nicholas's friends, and they all say the same thing. He worked alone. He sold good stuff. He didn't have any enemies—"

"He had one enemy," Marritt interrupted.

"If anyone knows who killed him," Dema continued, "they're not talking. Word must have gotten around that he's dead though. The superintendent says no one has buzzed his apartment for four or five days."

"That doesn't surprise me," the detective answered. "It's been two weeks since we found the body, and he was dead for three weeks before that. His phone has been disconnected for eight days. Anyone who doesn't know he's dead probably thinks he's moved, or else they've given up trying to reach him."

He waited for Dema to elaborate on his efforts.

"That's all," the rookie said. "Yesterday and the day before were my days off."

Marritt looked up at the ceiling. "You know something," he mused. "This office needs a good pinball machine."

Dema nodded.

"Except I'm not sure how the taxpayers would react. . . . What about the names in Doug Nicholas's address book. Anything new on them?"

"No, sir."

"Lemme see it."

Dema reached into his omnipresent manila folder and handed the black address book to his mentor. Marritt began thumbing through it.

"Hey! There's a page missing from this."

Dema's expression didn't change. "I noticed. It's been that way since we found it."

"You noticed? Well, why the hell didn't you say something? It's our first break."

"I doubt it."

"Jim, how can you miss it? Whoever killed Doug Nicholas had a last name that began with the initial —Shit! None of the names are in alphabetical order."

"I noticed that too," Dema answered. "Plus anyone who killed Doug Nicholas would have taken the whole book—that's if they'd seen it. There's no way they'd have stopped to look for the one page with their name on it."

"I guess that's right," Marritt grumbled. "Still, if there's a missing page, I'd like to know what's on it." Annoyed, he reached for the cup of coffee on his desk and brushed against an ashtray, sending it clattering to the floor. He groaned and was about to leave it lie when he remembered that, if he didn't clean up the mess, Dema would. Bending over, he coaxed the assorted butts and ashes onto a sheet of paper with the palm of his hand and dumped them in the wastepaper basket. Then, wiping his palm on the seat of his pants, he resumed questioning.

"What about Reuben, Matt—three-ten East Sixty-ninth Street?"

"Nothing," Dema answered. "I haven't talked to him yet."

"Well, when you do, say hello for me. I talked to his brother the other night, and I don't like the pattern I see unfolding."

"Meaning what?"

"I'm not quite sure. Right now, it's just a hunch, but give me a day or two and maybe I'll work it out. Meanwhile, what do you have that's new on our friend Agatha Tilden?"

"Not much," Dema answered. "She's lived in the building for two and a half years, always pays her rent on time, and is, quote, an ideal tenant, end quote. That's from the superintendent. Her family lives in Minnesota, and she goes home to visit once a year. I got that from a neighbor."

"Does she have any financial problems?"

"Apparently not. She makes three hundred a week as a day-care supervisor and her expenses are minimal."

"Was she in Doug Nicholas's address book?"

"Of course. She bought from him."

"What do you have on her friends?"

"The neighbors say they're ordinary. She usually has a boyfriend, although she changes them pretty often. That seems to be her choice rather than theirs."

"Anything else?"

"Nothing relevant. I put her name through the computers—criminal, hospital records, credit bureaus, the works. All that showed up was her driver's license and an abortion in early August.

Marritt looked toward the window, then at Dema. "Do we know the father?"

"What difference does it make?"

"Just a hunch." Slowly, the detective rose from his chair and began to pace. "Let's suppose for a moment that Doug Nicholas got Agatha Tilden pregnant. Let's also suppose that she wasn't too pleased with the whole matter. Maybe she flipped out."

"Meaning?"

"Meaning she went next-door one night and hacked him to pieces. It wouldn't be the first time in this city. And it would explain very nicely why she's been holding out on us." Bending forward, Marritt looked out the window at the gathering storm clouds. "Today's Sunday. Our friend Miss Tilden should be home. I think I'll pay her a visit."

Aggy reacted to the intercom buzz with a start, then lifted the receiver on her end to find out who was buzzing "Who is it?"

"Richard Marritt of the New York City Police Department. I'd like to talk with you, Miss Tilden."

She pushed the admit button and listened to the sound of Marritt's footsteps as he lumbered up the stairs. Then, opening the door before he knocked, she greeted him with a less than warm smile and began the conversation before he could: "We're more careful about locking the front door now, although I don't suppose it would have made any difference in Doug's case."

"Why do you suppose that, Miss Tilden?"

His accusatory tone caught her off guard. "I don't know," she answered. "I guess I just assumed that Doug knew the person who killed him."

"Why?"

Again, his tone of voice left her momentarily flustered. "Feminine intuition," she said at last with a flip of her head and a smile that came out more a grimace.

Marritt stared hard into her eyes, not quite certain what to say next. He never outlined interviews in advance, preferring to "wing it." Now, however, he wished he had prepared his attack a little more fully.

"Miss Tilden," he said at last, "I'll be very frank. We're up against a stone wall. We know Doug Nicholas was a dealer, and we're pretty sure that whoever killed him got over two hundred thousand dollars. We don't know who did it, and I think you can help us more than you have. I want every scrap of information you have on Doug Nicholas, and I want it now. What do you know about him?"

"Nothing more than I've already told you."

"Was he a well-behaved neighbor?"

"Yes."

"Did you know any of his friends?"

"You asked me that the other day, and I told you no."

"Did you ever go out with him?"

"No!"

The answer, Marritt thought, had come a little too quickly, and he decided to play on the agitation in her voice by making her wait for the next question.

Five seconds . . . ten seconds . . . "Did he ever ask you out?"

"No."

"But you've been in his apartment?"

"Once. I told you that."

"Only once?"

"That's all."

"Were you attracted to him?"

"That's none of your business."

"Or vice versa?"

"For Christ's sake," she snapped. "He was gay. Okay! Is that what you wanted to know?"

Marritt's eyes took on a questioning look. "Gay?"

"Yes, gay! You know. Homosexual. That's the word for people you cops call queers and faggots."

"I know what gay means, Miss Tilden. Why didn't you tell me this the other day?"

"Because I didn't think it was any of your fucking business."

Marritt exploded. "Look, you spoiled brat. A man has been murdered, I'm a cop, and my business is to find out who killed him. I don't care if he was heterosexual, bisexual, transsexual or the Pope. I want to find out who killed Doug Nicholas!"

The ferocity of his outburst took Aggy by surprise, and Marritt lowered his voice by several decibels. "You told us you were home every night the month Doug Nicholas was killed. What did you hear?"

"Nothing."

"I don't believe you."

She couldn't tell him. If she had gone to the police when she first realized what she had heard, it would have been all right. Now Marritt would know she had been holding back on him, and he would think she had been involved.

"I didn't hear anything," she said quietly. "I've told you that several times now."

"What did you smell in the hall for three weeks while your neighbor's body was rotting?"

"Nothing."

"What were his visitors like?"

"How should I know? I don't exactly stay up nights peeping through keyholes."

"Was Doug Nicholas strictly gay or bisexual?"

"To make a long story short, I don't want to talk about it."

"What was the nature of your relationship?"

"Did I fuck him," Aggy screeched. "Is that what you're asking? I fuck anybody I want."

Marritt turned his back and began to walk back and forth across the room. Fifteen seconds . . . Twenty . . . The Confederate cavalry cutlass on the wall seemed to jump out at him.

"Two can play this game," Aggy thought to herself. "I'll fix myself a gin and tonic and won't offer him one."

"Those are nice begonias on the mantelpiece, Miss Tilden."

Aggy didn't answer.

"I'm particularly interested in the cork panel underneath one of them." He turned to face her. "Where did it come from?"

Aggy looked nervously at the panel. "I found it about a month ago . . . by the trash can on the sidewalk."

Marritt lifted the panel at one end, knocking the potted begonia to the floor. Wordlessly, he carried it to the corridor, where he fished a skeleton key from his back pocket and pushed it into the newly installed lock on Doug Nicholas's door. Moments later, he returned.

"This panel belongs in the ceiling above the kitchen alcove in Doug Nicholas's apartment. I suggest you put it back, or you might get charged with petty larceny."

Aggy shook.

"I don't know what kind of game you're playing with us, Miss Tilden, but I don't like it. Someone has been killed. It could happen again."

"But—"

"Think about it. You'll be hearing from me shortly."

Marritt turned and walked toward the door. From behind, a low guttural sound punctured the air. Then, slowly, evenly, came the words—"Get . . . out . . . of . . . my . . . home."

"Anything you want, Miss Tilden. Have a good day."

And then he was gone. And Aggy was alone, her world upside down like a bizarre episode with a Presidential candidate pulling out a gun and shooting into the crowd. When would it end? Now, maybe . . . Everything was starting to fade.

CHAPTER 18

Monday morning. . . . The precinct house. . . . Ten o'clock.

"I'm in a foul mood," Marritt announced, "so look out."

"I'm used to it," Dema said.

"Yeah! Well, you ain't seen nothing compared to this." Wearily, the detective slumped behind his desk, took a cigarette from the top drawer, and lit it. "Christ! The week's just starting, and already things can't get any worse."

"What happened?"

"So much, I don't know where to begin. Two days ago, I saw this piece of moldy cheese lying on the kitchen counter, so I threw it out. This morning, the little one—he's seven—yells at me for ruining his chemistry experiment. Yesterday afternoon, I saw Agatha Tilden. I'll get to that one later. Five minutes ago, the desk sergeant tells me there's a rumor that some nut with a high-powered rifle is planning to shoot Santa Claus at the Macy's Thanksgiving Day Parade. That's right here in our precinct. I can see the headlines already—*Santa Shot Dead: Cops Ignored Informant's Tip.*"

Dema watched as a thin curl of smoke escaped the detective's lips.

"That's not all," Marritt muttered. "Coming in on the subway this morning, I read that the President wants to visit the South Bronx. What nonsense! He'll drive up in an armored car, pull two hundred cops away from their jobs for a police escort and then, when he goes back to Washington, he'll think he's seen the neighborhood. What they ought to do is give him a subway token and let him go up on his own. That'd be quite a trip."

Dema waited for the monologue to continue.

"I saw the President once," Marritt said. "Not the one we got now, but the one before him. I was on crowd-patrol duty when he came to a Chamber of Commerce luncheon in Manhattan. Six black limousines pulled up in front of the Waldorf, and a half dozen Secret Service men jumped out. Before we knew it, the President's car was surrounded by them. All we saw after that was a ring of Secret Service agents pushing toward the hotel. I think I saw the President's leg. Big fucking deal."

Leaning forward, the detective stubbed out his cigarette. "What the hell; it doesn't matter. What's really eating at me is Agatha Tilden. There's something about her I can't figure. I mean, on one level, she's belligerent as hell, but I can't help feeling that inside she's scared stiff."

"What's her problem?"

"I don't know. But I figure maybe you should go over and check her out. You're about her age. Maybe she'll relate better to someone from her own generation." Longingly, Marritt stared at his partially burned cigarette. "She'll be at the day-care center until four or four-thirty. Why don't you drop by her apartment sometime after that. Hell! Do a good job on this case, and maybe you'll make detective off it."

"I didn't know promotions were that easy."

"You'd be surprised. You know how I made detective? One night before a big drug raid up in Harlem, I got the bright idea of crawling into the basement of the target building and turning off the water pressure. That way, even though it took us twenty minutes to knock down the door, the pushers couldn't flush the stuff down the toilet. If I'd played my cards right, I could have made Commissioner off that case."

"Maybe you still will."

"Yeah! And maybe someday the Yankees will rehire Mel Allen."

* * *

Peering through the leaves of potted plants that hung by the large bay window in her apartment, Aggy saw that the sky was gray. For the second time in less than a week, she was spending a work day at home. The cork panel—where had it come from? "From the trash," she answered. "Are you sure?"

"Stop it!" she mumbled. "Stop talking to yourself."

The apartment had a sinister aura. "I'm not perfect," she whispered. "I've got problems like everyone else." What time was it? Four p.m. "I'm not crazy," she told herself. "I'm not."

Click.

"Oh, God!"

Click.

There it was again.

. . .

Aggy froze.

C-r-r-k.

Someone was trying to unscrew the lock on the door to her apartment.

Silence.

Nothing.

"Take a deep breath," she told herself. "Take a deep breath and—"

BZST!

The intercom.

"Get hold of yourself. . . . Just push the button and find out who it is, and—"

"Hello, Miss Tilden? This is James Dema of the New York City Police Department. I wonder if I could come upstairs for a moment."

Leaning against the wall for support, Aggy stared at the plants around the room. A lot of effort had gone into making them look the way they did. Most people didn't realize how much they changed the emotional impact of the apartment. Most people thought they just grew. That's what Rubes thought.

"Miss Tilden."

"What do you want?"

"I just told you. It won't take more than a few minutes. I have a couple of questions. That's all."

"Leave me alone," Aggy whispered. "I wish all of you would leave me alone."

"Miss Tilden?"

"All right! All right!"

She stabbed at the intercom button with her finger and missed.

"Miss Tilden, are you going to let me in or not?"

"Jesus! I said yes."

She hit at the buzzer a second time and held it firmly in place. A minute later, Dema appeared at the top of the stairs.

"I'm sorry to bother you," he began as she let him in. "I know this has been a difficult two weeks for you, but there are several questions I thought you might be able to answer."

He was taller than she was—by a lot. And his shoulders were broader than she had realized when they first met. Aggy waited.

"Actually, I didn't want to come. Lieutenant Marritt sent me."

His hair was light brown and wavy, his hands large and very strong. Where had she seen him before?

"I wonder if you could tell me a little more about the cork panel you found."

"I already told your detective friend, I found it in the trash outside the apartment. That's all I know about it."

Why was he looking at her that way?

"Are you certain?"

"Yes."

"All right. If that's all you remember, I'm sorry to have troubled you."

Would he really go that quickly? It didn't make sense.

A dark shadow was intruding from the corner of her mind.

"What do you want?" she blurted out.

"Pardon?"

"What do you want from me?"

"I told you, Miss Tilden. Lieutenant Marritt had a question he wanted me to ask."

"And?"

"I've asked it."

She had knocked. That was it! She had gone over to Doug's apartment, knocked on the door, and Doug had let her in. There was another man, sitting in the shadows, and she had felt she should leave; but the feeling passed and she'd gone in. . . . "What do you see in the darkness?"—"Cat's eyes." . . . Yes, he'd been introduced. Jim. She couldn't see his face, but the cat went to him, jumped onto his lap, and sat curled at his groin. And this man, Jim, hadn't moved except to stroke the cat, almost as though he was hiding. And she'd been uncomfortable because Doug wasn't gentle like she'd seen him before. He was tense and coiled and harsh and hard, and she'd thought maybe this man in the shadows was business, and then she'd realized that the man was Doug's lover.

"Miss Tilden."

Six weeks ago, a year . . . When had it been?

"Miss Tilden."

Aggy pressed a fist to her mouth and began to shake. Involuntarily, the words tumbled out: "I know you."

For a moment, there was silence. "That's right," Dema said at last in a low level voice. "And, if you know what's good for you, you'll stay out of this."

He was almost on top of her.

Just barely, she managed a response. "Is that a threat?"

"Yes."

CHAPTER 19

Aggy lay on the beach, unconscious, her body weighing heavily on the sand. A tall, blond doctor stood over her with Rubes at his side. "Don't let her talk," the doctor said. "If she does, she'll die."

The sun burned bright. It warmed her body and made her insides glow.

"She's awake now," said the doctor. "Let's hope, for her sake, that everything turns out all right."

Aggy sat up and opened her eyes. The ocean loomed nearby. "Look how bright the sun is," she whispered.

"Don't talk," the doctor warned.

"But I have to. Look at the sun. Everything is black and white."

Then her insides gave way. Her body opened and blood started to pour. Rubes was there, somewhere, she was sure of it, but he was kissing a headless corpse. Her parents were home. From her bedroom upstairs, she could hear their car in the driveway. Oh, God! There was blood all over. And someone was smashing her face again and again, and there were sirens and . . .

"Wake up! Wake up," she ordered. "You're dreaming. . . . Get hold of yourself. Find out where you are."

Frantically, Aggy thrashed her body from side to side, lashing out at the blankets twisted around her thighs. The siren was still wailing. "The mirror—I've got to get to the mirror to see my face!" Ripping the blankets aside, she tumbled out of bed and staggered to the bathroom. "My face!"

Slowly, she touched her hands to her lips, her cheeks and eyes, watching every move reflect off the mirror above the sink. Her features were in place.

What time was it? Morning, Tuesday, the day after Dema. Her disorientation was frightening. And then she realized the siren was still wailing, so she crossed to the window and looked down on the street. Two women stood at the curb, pointing to the hood of a gold Pontiac LeMans. "It's the theft alarm," one of them shouted, looking up toward Aggy. "It went off for nothing. Call the police."

Call the police! Right! "Hello, Officer Dema. This is Agatha Tilden. I wonder if you could put aside your hostilities long enough to do me a favor. No, it has nothing to do with your lover. You see—"

The intercom buzzed.

"Oh, Christ! What now?"

"Call the police," the woman on the street bellowed.

The siren kept wailing. Again, the buzzer.

"All right! All right!" Lurching to the intercom, Aggy lifted the receiver. "Who is it?"

"Delivery boy," a Hispanic voice answered.

"Delivering what?"

There was no response.

Still the siren. Then the buzzer, this time longer.

"Delivery boy."

"What do you want?"

"Flowers for Señorita Tilden."

"My name," Aggy told herself. "My name's on the mailbox in the vestibule next to the buzzer." Backing across the room to the window, she turned and looked out onto the street. There was no delivery van in sight. "Find someone else to mug, you prick."

Again the buzzer. "Señorita, I have flowers to deliver."

"I don't want them," she shouted. "Take them back."

"But, Señorita, I cannot do that."

"Then drop them at your feet."

From the street again. "Call the police."

Back to the window. "Call them yourself," Aggy shrieked.

The cutlass on the wall—God, what she could do with it . . . "No one in my family has ever committed suicide before. I'm going to be the first." . . . The walls were closing in on her. "I want to be outside where I can breathe. . . . Get dressed. I can't go outside without being dressed. . . . Put some clothes on."

The siren was still wailing. Aggy pulled on a sweater and jeans. Cautiously, because she hadn't forgotten the mugger, she opened the door and stepped into the long narrow corridor outside her apartment. A fluorescent bulb glowed overhead. The hallway carpeting was tattered and dark green. "One step at a time," she told herself. "Don't trip." Shakily, she clung to the banister on the stairs for support. "Okay! Ground floor. This is it."

Aggy opened the lobby door. On the vestibule floor, a dozen red roses lay carefully bunched with a small white card stapled to the wrapper. Still not believing, she knelt down and stared at the note attached:

I'm sorry if there are things about me that are wrong. In a lot of ways, I'm sorry for what I am. But I need you. You're the only important person who cares.

Love,
Rubes

"Oh, shit," she murmured. "Oh, shit, shit, shit!"

And then, suddenly, the day just done came into focus—the buzzer and the siren and the shouting and the dreams. "I'm going crazy," she said. "I really am. I need help."

And then she turned . . . back upstairs to her apartment . . . Next to the bed, a Manhattan telephone directory lay on the floor. . . . Hofflin . . . Hoffman . . . There it was—Hoffmann W N Dr . . . 225-3011.

Holding her breath, Aggy dialed. "My name is Agatha Tilden," she said when the answering-machine tape had run its course. My telephone number is 871-1672. I'd like Dr. Hoffmann to call me back as soon as possible."

CHAPTER 20

Pushing the papers on his desk aside, Marritt looked toward the office door. "Happy Wednesday," he grumbled as Dema entered. "Have a seat."

On cue, the rookie settled in a metal-framed chair opposite the detective. A smudge of mustard was visible just above Marritt's upper lip.

"How was your meeting the other night with Agatha Tilden?"

"So-so."

"Meaning what?"

"Nothing new," Dema answered. "I asked her about the cork panel, and she told me she'd found it in the trash."

"And after that?"

"That was it."

Slowly, as though with great effort, Marritt straightened up. "What do you mean, 'that was it'?"

"That was the only question I asked."

"I don't understand. You mean to tell me, you couldn't think of anything else?"

"I could have, but I figured what's the use. She wasn't talking."

The detective smiled. "Jim, I don't mean to imply anything, but have you by chance gotten to know our friend Miss Tilden a little more intimately than you're letting on?"

"No, sir."

"You're sure of that?"

Dema's face reddened. "Absolutely. Actually, I think she's a little nuts."

Marritt returned to a slouching position. "I guess that's right. Meanwhile, I just ate a ham sandwich that didn't agree with me."

The telephone rang, sparing Dema the need to answer. Marritt leaned forward to pick up the receiver, then ran a hand across the back of his neck. "Okay! Send him up."

"That was the desk sergeant," he told Dema when the receiver was back in place. "Arthur Nicholas—Doug Nicholas's father—is coming upstairs to see us."

The rookie stood up.

"Where the hell do you think you're going?"

"I don't know. I figured you'd want to talk with him alone."

"Not on your life. Besides, this is a part of the job you'll have to get used to sooner or later." Taking a deep breath, Marritt rose and crossed to the door. "Good afternoon," he said as Arthur Nicholas came into view. "I'm Richard Marritt. We tried to locate you, or any of Doug's relatives for that matter, but we didn't have much success. I'm glad you've gotten in touch with us."

The visitor put out his hand. He was balding and rather frail. Dema guessed that he was several years past sixty.

"Hello, Mr. Marritt. I'm Arthur Nicholas. I'm sorry you weren't able to get in touch with my wife or me. You see, we live in Pennsylvania and, well, I'm afraid we lost touch with our boy. We didn't learn about the tragedy until yesterday."

Marritt motioned for the guest to enter and take a seat. "Mr. Nicholas, this is James Dema. He's the patrolman I've assigned to the case, and he's been doing a good job. We haven't solved anything yet, but we do have a few leads."

The new arrival sat and looked down at his hands. "Do you know why it happened?"

Marritt tugged at his hair. "Do you know what your son's occupation was?"

"No, officer, I'm afraid I don't. I'm embarrassed to say this, but my wife and I haven't heard from our son for five years."

Dema looked self-consciously at the floor.

"Mr. Nicholas," Marritt began, "we have reason to believe that your son was engaged in the sale of illegal drugs. We think that someone who knew about this killed him for the money that was involved."

"Oh."

Marritt waited for something more, but nothing came.

"Has he been properly buried?" Arthur Nicholas asked at last.

"The authorities gave him a simple funeral. Everything that was necessary was done. Of course, if you'd like, the body can be exhumed and transported to Pennsylvania."

The man's voice grew shakier. "Thank you, officer. I'm very appreciative, but that won't be necessary." He paused. "Unless there's something more that I can do to help, I suppose I should go back home. I'm sorry if I caused you gentlemen any trouble."

A wave of embarrassment ran through Marritt's insides. The man's son had been butchered to death, he had just been forced to admit to two strangers that he hadn't heard from his boy in five years, and here he was apologizing for taking up ten minutes of their time. "That's all right," he said. "There's one other matter that might concern you, though. Your son did have some personal property at the time of his death. Not much—a stereo, two radios, a television. He also had a little under five hundred dollars in the bank. All of that belongs to you and Mrs. Nicholas."

Arthur Nicholas pondered his inheritance. "I really don't want it. Perhaps you could give it to charity."

"I'd be glad to. If you leave your address with the desk sergeant downstairs, we'll send you a release form in the mail."

The visitor from Pennsylvania walked to the door, then stopped. "You know," he said softly, "it's very strange. I remember the day my wife and I brought Doug home from the hospital as though it were yesterday. He was so small, with tiny hands and pink cheeks. . . . He had his whole life ahead of him. . . .

Neither cop spoke in the wake of Arthur Nicholas's departure.

"Does this mean we're at a dead end?" Dema asked at last.

Marritt didn't answer.

"I suppose not," the rookie answered his own question. "We still have Agatha Tilden. Do you really think she might have done it?"

"Not really," Marritt said finally. "If she'd done it, she wouldn't be using the cork panel from the kitchen alcove as part of her begonia garden."

"I guess that's right."

Marritt glanced at his watch. "It's three-thirty, and I get off duty at four. Let's have a beer."

"I'm on until eight," the rookie protested.

"Fuck it. I'm your boss, and I say let's have a beer. You can come back later and work till nine if you feel guilty about it."

They left the station house together and turned down Columbus Avenue, passing a small liquor store on the way. Marritt liked the store's proprietor. He always kept a pot of coffee and some donuts in a back room—free for cops. The arrangement worked well both ways. The cops got free food, and the proprietor benefited from a steady stream of uniformed policemen walking in and out of his store—the best police protection available.

"Do you know the bars in the neighborhood?" Marritt queried.

"No."

"There's a good one on Seventy-fifth Street. They don't hassle you about taking too much time, and the second beer is on the house if you're a cop. You want to go there?"

Dema stepped left to avoid a mound of trash on the sidewalk.

"You gotta watch where you go around here," Marritt continued. "Some of the bars are gay. If you walk inside by mistake, you feel like a weirdo."

Dema shrugged.

"Which reminds me," the detective said with sudden enthusiasm. "I forgot to tell you—Agatha Tilden says that Doug Nicholas was gay."

"I know."

Marritt cast a glance in his cohort's direction. "Well, why the hell didn't you tell me?"

"It didn't seem important. A couple of people I spoke with told me he was bisexual. I thought it was common knowledge."

"Well, it wasn't common knowledge to me," Marritt grumbled. "Look, Jim, this could give us a whole new angle. Doug Nicholas's bed was unmade when we found the body. He was stabbed close to a dozen times. If he was queer, maybe it was a crime of passion."

"You're forgetting one thing," Dema answered. "Someone took a panel out of the kitchen ceiling, and what we presume to be two hundred thousand dollars is missing. Also, the body was fully dressed, which means he wasn't in bed when it happened. I think robbery was the motive."

The tavern was only a half block away, and Marritt decided to let the matter drop. Reaching the front door, he held it open and gestured for his companion to go inside. "Is this all right?" he asked, pointing to a small table in the corner.

"Sure."

"The beer is nice and cold here, even in summer."

It was dark inside, and the detective banged his knee against a chair as he moved past the bar. Adjusting his eyes, Dema focused on a cracked bulletin board which listed the day's fare: "Burgers $1.55 . . . Fries 85¢."

Marritt sat at the table with his back to the wall and began gently massaging his injured knee. "This is a pretty good precinct we got here," he said at last. "I've been in some bad ones. I started out in the 28th Precinct up in Harlem, and I can count the number of good days I had there on one hand. Once we had a heroin scare—some guy who was selling bad heroin on the street—poison. The junkies bought it and were dropping like flies. Turns out this guy had been mugged by an addict, so to get even he decided to kill as many of them as possible by cutting heroin with cyanide and getting them to shoot it into their veins—not a bad idea, actually. The mob caught him before we did. This precinct is different. It's a good place to start. Central Park West and Riverside are nice streets. Columbus and Amsterdam are getting better, and West End is good."

Dema looked at his mentor. "If West End was so

good, we wouldn't be sending Doug Nicholas's typewriter to the Salvation Army."

A waitress came and Marritt ordered two beers, then turned back to face Dema.

"Look, let me give you some free advice. Save your sympathy for yourself. You'll need it someday. If you want to worry about something, worry about how ten years from now you'll have to send two kids through school on a cop's salary when you're not on the take and you're too tired to moonlight at night. Save your sympathy for some colored kid up in Harlem who's too short to play basketball and can't hit like Willie Mays. The only recruiter coming after him is the United States Army."

The beers came.

"You fool around with women much?" Marritt queried.

"A little."

"That's good. You're single. You can enjoy it. I suppose I could, but I don't."

"How come?"

"I got the family—the wife and the two kids." Marritt leaned forward in his chair. "The funny thing is, after all these years, I still love 'em. I'll tell you something. Being a cop, you get kicked around a lot. Once, about five years ago, I thought of switching. I figured I was only thirty-five and maybe I'd get a different job. You know, a shopkeeper or an accountant or something. I couldn't do it. I'd never gone past high school, and no one would take a guy thirty-five who didn't have training. It stank. Here I was, forty years from the grave, and my whole life was already laid out like concrete. I had a wife and two kids, so I couldn't go back to school. I was a cop, and none of it could ever change. It shouldn't be that way."

Marritt took a shlurp of beer. "I'll tell you something. My kids won't be cops. I'm paying two thousand dollars a year tuition for the two of them, so they can go to a decent school. They're all that matters."

The waitress brought a small dish of shelled peanuts and placed them in the center of the table. Dema started on his beer.

"You got a family?" Marritt asked.

"My father's dead," the rookie answered. "My mom lives in Brooklyn, and I got a sister in Chicago who's married with a kid."

"What did your dad do?"

"He worked for the Parks Department. And he hung around the Democratic clubhouse a lot hoping for something better, but nothing ever came."

"That's politics," Marritt advised. "I never had much use for it. Things were kind of fun when Kennedy was President. Those fifty-mile hikes; that guy who did the Kennedy imitation on records; and Kennedy did some good things for labor. But, since then, forget it."

Raising his hand, Marritt signaled the waitress for another beer. Dema popped a peanut in his mouth and offered the dish to his drinking partner. "No thanks," the detective answered. "I'm on a diet. . . . At least I should be. I don't need peanuts on top of beer."

"I thought all baseball fans ate peanuts," Dema chided.

"I suppose so, but things are changing. Even baseball's changing. I was talking with my kids the other day. The older boy's nine; the little one is seven. Neither of them had ever heard of the Brooklyn Dodgers. Can you imagine that? Roy Campanella . . . Carl Furillo . . . Jackie Robinson . . . The older one thought they used to play in Los Angeles. The little one hadn't heard of them at all. Kids growing up today think of the Brooklyn Dodgers the same way we looked at the old New York Highlanders when we were kids."

Dema smiled.

"Let's face it," the older cop continued. "Kids are changing too. Last week, the older one was eating spaghetti with his fingers, so I told him to get a fork. You know what he told me? Eating spaghetti with your fingers helps break down barriers. And it makes it easier to get in touch with the spaghetti. Meanwhile, the little one likes to jump off stone walls holding an open umbrella over his head."

"Times change."

"I know . . . I know . . . But thank God, some things stay the same. Kids still play baseball with imaginary runners when there aren't enough boys for a full game. . . . Both my kids get a kick out of going to the zoo to feed the ducks. . . . Neither of them will go to bed without a night light. . . . And my wife still tells them not to wear torn underwear in case they're in an accident and get taken to a hospital where some doctor looks at them. I don't know why that's important, but my mother used to tell it to me too."

"So did mine."

"So did everybody's."

The detective looked down at his watch. "I got to go," he said suddenly. "The little one is in a play at school tonight in the role of Button Gwinnett. That's some guy who signed the Declaration of Independence. I can't miss it." He took three dollar bills from his pocket and laid them on the table. "The drinks are on me."

As they left the bar, Marritt turned south. Central Park West and 72nd Street was the nearest subway stop. He'd be home in forty minutes, and at the play by the time the curtain rose. The subways generally got him where he wanted to go on time. By now, he was even used to the filth.

Back in the sixties, on the night of the power blackout when hundreds of trains had stalled beneath the streets, Marritt had been sent into the tunnels on rescue duty. He had one high-powered flashlight to guide him. Halfway into the first tunnel, he realized that he was wading through rats. The subway tunnels were their home. Marritt spent nine hours in the tunnels that night guiding people to safety. A dozen years later, during the blackout of 1977, he volunteered for the same job all over again.

Marritt flashed his pass to the woman on duty by the subway platform and boarded a downtown local. At 59th Street, he changed to the express. He hoped the play was good. The little one only had two lines to speak but, at the end of Act Two, he got to sign the Declaration of Independence.

The family was really all that mattered. Life could be rough. There were times he had been forced to accept inequity and defeat but, on balance, things weren't bad. Hell, it didn't even matter that he'd had seven homicides this year and hadn't solved any of them. Maybe he'd get lucky on the next one.

CHAPTER 21

It was a half hour later than he usually left work, and Matt didn't feel up to the hassle of the subway. Too much was weighing on his mind, and the last thing he needed was a bunch of assholes jamming their elbows into his ribs. At Avenue of the Americas and 44th Street, he hailed a cab.

"Where are you going?" the driver asked.

"Sixty-ninth Street, just off Second Avenue."

"You mind if I ride with the meter off?"

Matt looked at the man behind the wheel. "How much will it cost?"

"Whatever you think is fair, buddy."

"I'll give you three dollars."

"You got a deal."

The cab moved up the cavern of Sixth Avenue, then into Central Park. Matt rolled down the window and stared out at the autumn leaves. The park was one of the few outdoor spots left to enjoy in New York but, at times, it seemed an endangered species on the verge of being crushed by giant buildings pushing in from either side.

There had been one moment of absolute freedom in Matt's life. Years before, the summer after his senior year at Princeton, he had pulled some clothes together and thumbed his way across the country. For four months, he had traversed the continent—out to California, then back again. Stopping in small towns—Glenn's Ferry, Idaho; Williams, Arizona. . . .

Camping in canyons and on the range. . . . He had moved at his own pace, sometimes staying in one place for a week, sometimes moving on inside of a day. In northern Oregon, he had stood for hours on a rock jutting out into the Pacific Ocean as the waves broke dangerously close, washing over his feet and stinging his face with spray. Then, inch by inch, the tide receded until Matt, looking out at the setting sun, felt he had won the right to stay.

In the midst of it all, there had been one timeless moment when everything came together. It was a summer afternoon in New Mexico. The sun was warm and the sky a perfect blue. Thirty miles west of Albuquerque, the trucker who was giving him a lift turned south and let him off at the side of the road. Matt watched the truck fade into the distance, then realized that, for the first time in his life, he was completely alone. All around him, as far as the eye could see, there were colors. No people . . . no cars . . . nothing but color. Ridges . . . rocks . . . plateaus . . . and the open spaces between them. Greens . . . blues . . . brown and red. He had never experienced anything like that moment before or since. For the first and only time in his life, he had felt free.

The cab turned onto 69th Street and pulled to a stop in front of the large high-rise building marked "310." Matt handed the driver three dollars and slammed the car door behind him. Inside the lobby, he nodded to the doorman and took the elevator upstairs. He had just begun to change out of his gray tweed suit when the doorbell rang. "Just a minute," he called, rebuckling his belt. "Who is it?"

It rang again.

"Okay, okay! I'm coming."

Turning the inside lock, Matt opened the door and measured the tall, sandy-haired man in front of him.

"Hi! My name is James Dema. I'm with the New York City Police Department. Is it all right if I come in?"

Matt glanced at his watch. "Sure, but I don't have much time. I've got a class at eight."

"It won't take that long," the cop assured him. "I just want to ask you a few questions." Not waiting for a further invitation, he stepped inside. The room was dominated by a tan velvet sofa set on a brown area rug with chrome-armed chairs to the side. A highly polished mahogany wall unit housing an aquarium, books and a stereo system covered the far wall. Adjacent to it, Dema noted a glass dining table with bentwood chairs. "You have a nice apartment," he said.

"Thanks." Matt didn't like strangers in his living room, but discretion was the better part of valor. "Would you like a beer?"

"No thanks. I'm on duty."

"How about a Pepsi or Coke?"

"No thank you."

Dema continued to survey the room, focusing his attention on the aquarium. "That's quite a tank," he said, bending forward for a closer look. "How big is it?"

"Thirty gallons."

"What kind of fish?"

"They pretty much cover the lot. A couple of swordtails, black mollies, a few angelfish and some neon tetras. One or two scavengers to pick up the food on the bottom."

Dema bent down for a closer look. "That's a betta fish on the side, isn't it?"

Matt watched as the cop peered into the blue green water. This was small talk. He knew from experience when he was being manipulated.

"Right you are," he said with a grin. "What can I do for you?"

"You've got a dead swordtail in back," the cop said, ignoring the question.

Peering into the water, Matt saw the fish floating on its side, caught in the reeds midway between the water's surface and the tank's colored-gravel floor. Wordlessly, he reached for the miniature net by the tank's side and dipped it into the water. As the remaining fish darted away, he scooped the dead swordtail up and carried it into the bathroom. Dema heard the toilet flush. Then Matt reappeared through the bathroom door.

"I'll tell you why I'm here," the cop said. "Two and a half weeks ago, we found the body of a man named Doug Nicholas. He'd been stabbed to death maybe three weeks before that in his apartment on West End Avenue. Doug Nicholas was a dealer. He sold grass, hash and assorted other drugs. When we searched his apartment, we found an address book with your name in it."

Matt said nothing.

Dema raised his eyes level with those of his host. "Did you know him?"

"Yes."

"Could you tell me about him?"

Matt looked at the cop. "I'll be glad to help, but I'm not particularly anxious to get in trouble. You won't hold this against me, will you?"

"Not that I know of."

Matt smiled. "What I mean is, will I get busted if I tell you that I bought some grass?"

Dema smiled back. "That's not what I came for. We're investigating a murder. As far as I'm concerned, what you smoke is your own business."

Matt loosened up a little. "I bought some grass

from Doug Nicholas a few months ago. It was good stuff. I paid him eighty dollars and that was it."

"Where did you buy it?"

"At his apartment."

"Who put you in touch with each other?"

Matt hesitated. There was no need to drag Rubes into this. "I met him at a party on the Lower East Side. It was in a loft. You know, one of those old industrial buildings that's been converted for residential use. A bunch of us from the office went down after work. All totaled, there must have been about a hundred and fifty people there. I met Doug Nicholas in the crowd."

"How often did you buy from him?"

"Just once."

"Did you know he was dead?"

"I read it in the paper on Columbus Day. I remember the morning because we had the day off."

"Do you have any idea why someone killed him?"

Matt ran the question through his mind, weighing what he had already been told by Rubes and Aggy. "No, but my brother has a friend who lives in the same building Doug lived in. She said the police told her there was a lot of money in the apartment."

The cop raised his eyes slightly. "Would that be Miss Tilden?"

"Right."

"What do you know about her?"

"Not much," Matt answered. "I've only met her a few times. She seems nice enough."

"Do you know whether or not she was friendly with Doug Nicholas?"

"I think they were neighbors, nothing more."

"Have you talked with her about the murder?"

"Not really. She was pretty upset when I saw her, and I didn't want to make things worse."

"Did she tell you anything about the murder?"

"Not that I can remember."

"What are her living habits?"

"That's a strange question," Matt thought. "Could you be a bit more specific?"

"Is she generally home alone at night?"

"I wouldn't know."

"What did she tell you about the police investigation?"

"We haven't discussed it."

Dema took a long look at his host.

"He's nervous," Matt realized. "I don't know why, but he's nervous, maybe even scared."

"Where do you work?" Dema pressed.

"I'm in advertising."

"What kind?"

"Marketing research."

"You got big clients?"

"Pretty good. I work for one of the agencies."

"They pay you well?"

"Thirty-four thousand."

The cop took a pad from his left rear pocket and jotted, "$34,000." "That's not bad," he said, eyes still on the pad. "Of course, after taxes it's probably not so much."

The questions were starting to make Matt uncomfortable. "It's okay. How much do you make?"

"Sixteen five."

"With or without graft?"

Dema didn't answer.

Now the shoe was on the other foot. "You been on the force long?" Matt prodded.

"About a year."

"I didn't know they let rookies go out and interview people like this."

"My boss lets me."

The tables were turning in Matt's favor.

"How come you're a cop, anyway? You seem like a bright guy. You could be a travel agent or a maitre d' in a restaurant or something like that. Maybe even go to the City University and sell insurance."

"I like the job."

"Isn't it dangerous?"

Matt had won. Dema looked at his watch. "It's seven-thirty, and you said you had an appointment at eight. I won't keep you any longer." He got up to leave, then stopped. "Could you do me a favor?" he asked suddenly.

"Sure, what is it?"

"I know this sounds strange, but could you not tell your brother and Miss Tilden that I was here this evening?"

"That's an odd one," Matt thought to himself. "All right, but why not?"

Dema scratched his head. "Well, to tell you the truth, we don't think Miss Tilden has been completely honest with us. There's certain evidence which suggests that she knows more about this entire matter than she's told us to date—no hard proof, mind you, but we'd like to keep our options open."

Matt looked at the cop. "What sort of evidence?"

"It doesn't really matter. The important thing is that she cooperate with us in the long run. I'm sure she will."

"And besides," the cop added to himself, "I need time to defuse the time bomb that's ticking away in her head before it explodes."

CHAPTER 22

At least she was resilient, Aggy told herself; perhaps not the ultimate in stability but, for the time being, she'd let Dr. Hoffmann deal with that. "Just concentrate on trying to function." That was what he had told her. "Keep calm, settle back into your routine, and relax. I'll see you again tomorrow."

"Okay," Aggy told herself. "It's now seven-thirty; I'm home; I'm reasonably calm; and I'm hungry. Put all of that together and—oh, shit! It's Wednesday; I'm supposed to be at the museum tonight."

If the class was as boring as last week's, she didn't want to go. "Should I? No! The course stinks. . . . But I paid forty dollars for it. And maybe it will be better this time. . . . All right. I'll go, but, if it's boring, I'm walking out."

Her decision made, Aggy pulled a coat from the closet and trod downstairs to the street. West End Avenue was almost deserted, and she decided to walk up Broadway instead. Past a hardware store and supermarket; stopping to look at the window of a recently opened boutique. On the corner of Broadway and 79th, a tall gangly youth approached, wheeling a shiny ten-speed bicycle.

"Hey, lady! Wanna buy a bike?"

Aggy ignored him.

"Hey, lady! Whatsa matter? These are good wheels."

"Put it back where you stole it."

"Yeah! I'll put you someplace, like with a fist in your face."

Before she could answer, he walked off. "More excitement on the streets of New York," she told herself. She wasn't sure why she was going to the museum; maybe it had something to do with Matt.

A well-dressed man in his early thirties stood on the sidewalk less than a block ahead. As Aggy passed, he followed, catching up and casting a sideways glance. His tie was dark, with evenly spaced silver stripes. "Hi! How are you tonight?"

"Fine," she answered.

"It's a nice night."

Aggy kept walking.

"My name is Bruce."

"Bruce, do you always talk to strange women on the street?"

"Only the good-looking ones."

"Well, do me a favor—fuck off!"

Bruce left. The museum loomed straight ahead. Aggy made her way inside, past an American Indian exhibit to the second-floor lecture hall where her class met. The lecture had just begun. She looked around from the back of the room—no Matt.

". . . Last week, you will recall, we touched on incidents of communal jealousy among the Lugbara tribesmen of Central Africa. Tonight, we move to a fascinating case study from fourteenth-century Rheims. The allegation of sorcery was made by the uncle of . . ."

"Shit," she muttered. "I really don't need this." Annoyed, she turned and walked downstairs to the lobby, where she came face-to-face with her erstwhile classmate.

"Class over already?" Matt asked.

"You're late."

"I know, but only by five minutes. How come you're leaving?"

Aggy shrugged. "It started out as bad as last week."

For a moment, they exchanged looks, two people acknowledging the enemy in each other and making friends with it.

"So you're leaving?"

"Right."

"Would you like company?"

"All right."

Matt furrowed his brow just a bit. "I'm really not hungry. Why don't we go back to my place for a drink?"

Long pause.

"Should I?" she wondered. . . . "Okay, but just a drink," she answered.

They left the museum together and hailed a taxi.

"How was your day?" Matt asked when they were safely ensconced in the backseat.

"Not bad. I saw a shrink."

"No kidding! Why do that?"

"By now, I'd have thought it was obvious. I don't like getting up in the morning. I'm afraid to go to sleep at night. I want to find out what's in my head and get the whole thing over with."

Intrigued, Matt pursued the subject. "Can a psychiatrist help?"

"I think so. Anyway, I liked this one enough to make another appointment for tomorrow. He has a free hour at the end of the day."

"Did you tell him about the murder?"

"A little. We only had fifty minutes. Dr. Hoffmann—that's his name—Dr. Hoffmann thinks I'm a prime candidate for hypnosis."

Matt's voice underlined his skepticism. "I thought

that sort of stuff was reserved for museum courses on witchcraft, magic and sorcery."

"So did I," Aggy admitted, "but Dr. Hoffmann says it might work. Hypnosis is used for all sorts of things—to control smoking and overeating; as a cure for people who are afraid of public speaking or heights. My case fits into an area called time regression. And if I really heard what went on across the hall, then it isn't even a question of dredging up hundreds of childhood memories and interpreting them. It's a matter of remembering a specific incident that occurred not too long ago."

"Does this doctor think you really heard it?"

"He isn't sure."

"And you?"

Aggy paused, weighing her thoughts. "I don't know everything that happened," she said at last. "But I'm sure now that the things I do remember are real."

"What makes you so certain?"

"The images. Not so much the images, even, as the sounds. The blood and forms are still blurred in my mind, but the sounds are clear. Doug asking, 'What do you want?' and complaining that it was three o'clock in the morning. That was real. I heard it."

The cab pulled to a halt in front of Matt's building, and they got out. Through the lobby; up the elevator. "Why am I doing this?" Aggy wondered. "Do I really want to hurt Rubes this much?"

At the door to his apartment, Matt fumbled for his keys and let her in. The living room was nicer than she had expected, put together with considerable care and taste. "Maybe he's not so bad after all," she told herself. "Relax!"

"Let me take your coat," Matt offered.

She gave him her jacket, and he hung it next to his in the hall closet.

"Would you like a drink?"

"I don't know. What are you offering?"

"Scotch, bourbon, beer, soda; you name it. There's some grass if you'd like."

"I'll take a beer."

"All right." Matt disappeared into the kitchen and returned moments later with a bottle of Michelob. "Let me get you a glass and we'll be all set."

"Aren't you having anything?"

"If you don't mind, I'll smoke." Not waiting for an answer, he ducked back into the kitchen, then reappeared with a tall frosted glass in one hand and a tightly rolled joint in the other. "It's funny," he told her. "Beer mugs and marijuana both keep better in the freezer."

They settled on the sofa at a discreet distance from one another. Aggy took a sip of Michelob. Matt reached into his pocket for a book of matches and lit the joint. "You want some?" he asked, holding the butt end out.

"No thanks."

"If you change your mind, holler."

The room was dimly lit. The blinds were open, but no light was coming in from the street.

"So . . . ," Matt said, leaning back against the sofa. "Welcome to three-ten East Sixty-ninth."

"Thanks."

"What made you come?"

"I felt like it."

Easily, he took a drag on the joint. "I'm glad you're here, but I'll confess to being mystified as to what brought you. I don't think you like me very much."

"You've noticed."

"Where are you coming from?"

"You wouldn't understand."

"Try me. I'm smarter than I look."

Aggy smiled. Matt held out the joint, and she shook her head. "Tell me," she said. "How do I compare with The Blonde?"

"I wouldn't know. I haven't kissed you."

She was balancing on an emotional highwire without any net. "Is that the only way you have to compare us?"

"You're smarter than she is," Matt added.

"I won't argue with that."

"And better looking."

Aggy took a sip of beer and didn't answer, letting the comment dangle.

"I suppose you had an idyllic Midwestern childhood," Matt said, seeking to start her talking again.

"Guess again."

"What was wrong with it?"

"The usual—growing pains . . . academic adjustment . . . men who weren't interested in anything but a good fuck. When I was a sophomore at Barnard, I had a vaginal infection and wasn't allowed to sleep with anyone for twelve weeks. It might have been the best twelve weeks of my life."

Matt took another toke on the joint. "When did you and Rubes meet?"

"Right after that."

"And?"

"We went out a few times; that was it. Two months ago, we ran into each other on the street."

"How often do you see each other?"

"Now and then."

"Is there a future?"

"I doubt it."

Matt shifted position on the sofa, resting his arm just short of Aggy's shoulder. "Rubes thinks I did it," he said.

"Did what?"

"Killed Doug Nicholas."

"Did you?"

He laughed. "That wasn't the reaction I expected."

"What did you expect?"

"I don't know. I guess I thought you'd tell me that Rubes was ridiculous."

Again, Aggy put the beer to her lips. "Why does he think you did it?"

"I don't know. Some nonsense about how he could tell by watching my eyes the night we had dinner at your place. Maybe it was something you said that touched him off."

Aggy didn't answer.

"What *do* you remember about the murder?"

"Only what I told you and Rubes at dinner that night."

"What else?" Matt pressed.

"Zilch."

"Are you sure?"

"The way you push, you remind me of my father."

"I'm flattered."

"Don't be," she answered. "He and I don't get along as well as you might think. To give you an example, last winter for my twenty-fifth birthday, he gave me a pair of solid-gold pierced earrings."

"What's wrong with that?"

"I don't have pierced ears."

Matt relit the joint and took a toke. "Hey," he said suddenly, "I've got a question for you. Which king in a deck of cards doesn't have a moustache?"

"I wouldn't know."

"Which jack?"

"Same answer."

"Too bad. You just flunked the trivia intelligence test."

"How about The Blonde? Did she do any better?"

Gently, Matt reached out and touched a hand to Aggy's cheek. "I don't understand why you're talking to me like this."

"Don't worry. Sooner or later, you'll catch on."

"Do you want to go to bed?"

"I haven't decided yet."

His arms looked strong, and he had a lot more muscles than Rubes did. "I wonder what he'd be like to kiss."

Matt's finger traced along the side of her face, continuing down to the top button on her blouse.

"Do it," she said.

Then everything happened all at once. Matt held her face with both hands and took her mouth with his lips. His body pressed hard against her breasts, and he leaned down on top of her with his weight. But it was all wrong. It wasn't what she wanted. He was arousing her anger more fiercely than her desire, and suddenly she was struggling, pushing him away, pleading with him to stop. And when he didn't, she fought and kicked and scratched until—

"Jesus! What's the matter with you?"

"Get the fuck off me!" she shrieked.

And then they were on the floor, with Aggy rolling away . . . frightened, angry . . . She rose up, stumbled to the kitchen, and turned the water on hard. She drank with her mouth at the faucet, then wiped her face on her sleeve.

"I'm leaving," she said.

"Hey, I'm sorry."

"Don't worry about it. We made a mistake. That's why pencils have erasers."

"Look, I don't want you to go like this."

"I just told you, don't worry about it. If anyone asks, we'll call it a draw."

Silence.

"Your coat's in the closet," Matt said at last. "I'll get it."

"Don't bother. I can find my own way out."

"All right! Anything you want."

She found it and left.

Shaken, Matt crossed to the bathroom and looked in the mirror. A slight swelling was visible just beneath his left eye. A small scratch had begun to clot on the downside of his cheek. "She's crazy," he said out loud. "A goddamn crazy bitch."

He'd keep an eye on her, and wait.

CHAPTER 23

Still shaken, Aggy arrived at Dr. Hoffmann's office for her second visit the following afternoon at four o'clock. She felt funny sitting in a psychiatrist's waiting room. There was something gimmicky about it, and the whole thing smacked of failure—an admission of her inability to cope. So she sat there, feeling awkward, letting her eyes wander.

The office had obviously once been a residential apartment. The room she was in was a living room, sunken two steps from the foyer. It had old wooden arm chairs, a table with ten psychology books nestled together, and another table with a huge doll's house on top. Aggy looked around for dolls, but there weren't any.

"Does he have child patients?" she wondered. She tried to imagine an infant lying on a couch but, like babies who wear glasses, it was too incongruous. "He probably shrinks his patients and makes them live in the doll's house," she decided. And then she thought, "Someday, I'll have to write a story about a shrink. Better yet, a movie. The bludgeoned body of a beautiful young rape-murder victim is found in her apartment and, next to her, a pad with the words in her own handwriting—'The rapist, W. N. Hoffmann, 44 West 63rd Street.' That's a little cruel to Dr. Hoffmann," she thought, "but c'est la vie. Anyway, everyone can go after Dr. Hoffmann. He'll be arrested, tried and convicted. After he's been electrocuted, the district attorney who handled the case can realize that what the victim actually wrote on the pad was 'Therapist, W. N. Hoffmann, 44 West 63rd Street'—not 'The rapist,' 'Therapist.' Too bad for Dr. Hoffmann."

"Words are funny," she told herself. Therapist . . . rapist . . . "Devil" was "lived" spelled backwards for whatever that was worth.

The door to the waiting room opened and Dr. Hoffmann emerged. He was a tall, gray-haired man of about fifty. His looks had pleased Aggy the first time they met, and now they were equally reassuring. "Maybe I should ask him about my relationships with men," she thought.

"Come in, Miss Tilden. I'm delighted to see you."

Aggy walked self-consciously into the office and sat in an overstuffed chair with her back to the window. On her first visit, she had expected a couch and was surprised by its absence. Now she was comfortable with the chair. A couch would have left her feeling more helpless than she already did.

"How are you this afternoon?" he asked.

"All right, I guess."

"You shouldn't guess. The matter of how you are is important to both of us, so I'll ask you again, this time in a clearly professional capacity, how are you this afternoon?"

"Very upset," she answered, "as I'm sure you can tell. I don't know what I heard or when I heard it, but I'm hopeful that you can help me. I want to know what's going on inside my head."

Dr. Hoffmann smiled reassuringly. "Maybe I can help, maybe not. A psychiatrist can do only so much. He can only advise. I can try to help you help yourself, but I cannot remember for you. I can't tell you what's inside your head. The most I can do is help you to relax so you might remember. That's the purpose of the hypnosis we spoke about yesterday."

"How does it work?"

"By coupling relaxation of the body with total alertness of the mind. It's not uncommon for a person to suppress unpleasant occurrences that interrupt sleep. The most common example is children who hear their parents fighting late at night and remember nothing on a conscious level the following morning. What we will attempt this afternoon is a regression in time."

"Will it work?"

Dr. Hoffmann smiled. "Only time will tell. Not everyone is susceptible to the technique, and there's a great deal about it we don't know. Even its practitioners disagree as to whether regression involves reexperiencing an earlier event or simply remembering it."

"What do you think?"

"The latter. And hopefully yours will be an easy regression. "We're only going back five or six weeks to an event close to your consciousness. Now I'd like you to relax and take six deep breaths. . . . It's important that you pay the strictest attention. By that, I don't mean that you should grit your teeth. I want you to relax and block everything out of your mind except my voice and this gold chain."

"Can I blink?"

"Don't talk. Just be natural. Now let's start again. Six deep breaths. Now close your eyes and imagine the chain."

She couldn't concentrate.

"Yield," he said. "Imagine the chain as it swings back and forth. Pretend you're in a movie theater. Whatever you see on the screen is what actually happened. Imagine the chain. Watch it closely. Follow its motion through each arc. You are an ideal patient. I want you to keep watching closely."

In little more than a minute, Aggy was in a hypnotic state. Dr. Hoffmann emitted a sigh of satisfaction and began to probe.

"What is the dominant color in your mind, Miss Tilden?"

"Red."

"What kind of red is it? The red of a rose?"

"No." Her voice rose slightly. "It's blood."

"Whose blood?"

"I don't know. It's all over. It's on the floor . . . my face, it's everywhere."

"Whose blood is it, Miss Tilden?"

No answer.

"Is it your own?"

"No. It's someone else's. But it's all over me."

"Do you hear anything?"

No answer.

"Listen carefully. Do you hear anything?"

"I hear sounds."

"What kind of sounds?"

No answer.

"What time is it?"

"It's three o'clock in the morning."

"How do you know that?"

"He said so. Someone just said, 'It's three o'clock in the morning.' "

"Who said it?"

"I don't know. I think it was Doug."

"How many people are there with him?"

"One."

"Are you sure?"

"Yes."

"Is it a man or a woman?"

"A man."

"How do you know?"

"I can hear him."

"What's his name?"

"I don't know."

"What does he look like?"

"I don't know . . . I . . . I can't remember."

"Why can't you remember?"

No answer.

"Do you want to remember?"

"No."

"Why not?"

"Because I'm frightened."

"Why are you frightened?"

"Something's going to happen."

"What?"

"I don't know. Something awful."

"What's going to happen?"

No answer.

"I want you to listen carefully and describe for me everything that happens as it occurs."

"They're arguing with each other. Doug is backed up against the wall. 'What are you doing here? . . . What do you want? . . .' It's getting worse." Aggy's head swung from side to side. "He'll be killed." Tears gushed down the side of her face. "It's getting worse."

"What's getting worse?"

"It's getting worse . . . *I MADE IT UP!*" she screamed. "*IT'S ALL A DREAM.*"

Dr. Hoffmann leaned back and stared at the woman in front of him. She was sitting there, suddenly quite lucid and calm. The hypnotic trance was broken, but there was no sign of a release. There had been no catharsis, no cleansing of the soul. For a moment, he weighed the wisdom of his thoughts. Then, slowly, he began to speak.

"What I am about to say, Miss Tilden, might seem highly out of place in a profession where patients are expected to seek and find their own truths, but I will tell you something quite sincerely. I do not believe that what you have just recounted for me was a dream, and I think you know that. You are a very frightened woman, and that fear is justified. Somewhere inside, I am convinced, you know who murdered Doug Nicholas."

CHAPTER 24

For the second time in as many days, Richard Marritt was at the Empire Tavern with Dema as his drinking companion. This time though, the detective resented it. The police department was supposed to be a closely knit organization. If a cop had something to say, he should say it, and any fellow officer should be allowed to listen. It annoyed him that Dema had asked for an audience "in private." Whatever the rookie had to say, it had better be good. Yet here they were, sitting at the same table they'd sat at the day before, and Dema couldn't get off the ground.

"How was the play last night, sir? The one with Button Gwinnett."

"Very enjoyable."

Long pause.

"Did Mrs. Marritt like it?"

"She did."

Marritt wondered how long it would take the rookie to get to the point. He wasn't going to help him.

"I'm glad you enjoyed it," the young man said, squirming uncomfortably.

Slowly but surely, Marritt sensed his own annoyance giving way to concern. Old softie that he was, he couldn't let the kid dangle much longer.

"Jim, are you all right?"

"I suppose so," the rookie answered. "It's just that something has been bothering me about this case from the beginning."

"Can you put your finger on it?"

"Yes, sir."

"Let's have it."

Dema brushed an imaginary crumb from the surface in front of him and looked across the table at his mentor.

"Doug Nicholas used to be a friend of mine. That's why I volunteered for the assignment."

Marritt raised his eyebrows. "How good a friend?"

"He was my lover."

Long silence. Marritt opened and closed his mouth, but no words came out.

Dema resumed speaking. "It was a while ago; before I joined the force. I'm not apologizing. Nothing I did was wrong. But I felt I should tell you, since I'm working on the case. You might feel that, because of my past involvement, there's a professional conflict."

"Professional conflict," Marritt muttered incredulously. "Is that the only problem you think you have?"

"Yes, sir. I know there are people who might feel otherwise, but I hope you're not one of them."

"Professional conflict? . . . Oh, Christ."

"Look," Dema said, his voice toughening slightly. "I know what you're thinking. You hate it. That's nothing new to me. Parents hate it. Friends hate it. Sometimes I hate it. But I'm a good cop, and you know it."

There was no answer.

"I'm a good cop."

"What the hell does that have to do with it?"

"Everything." Dema's voice was hard now. "My personal life shouldn't make a difference."

"Maybe not, but it does."

"Only if *you* say so. You're the only one on the force who knows."

Marritt stared down at the back of his hands. "Are you still, what's the word, practicing?"

"Yes, sir."

"Have you considered seeking psychiatric help?"

"I don't want it."

"Not even for the sake of your own happiness?"

"I'm probably as happy as you are."

Marritt scraped his foot along the sawdust on the floor. The waitress hovered nearby, waiting for an order. The detective waved her off. "How come you're telling me this now?"

"I don't know. It bothered me, I guess."

"It bothers me too, just so you know it."

"It's working," Dema thought. "He's taking it at face value."

"Even if I didn't care about your sexual orientation, you've been holding out on me and I don't like it."

"I'm sorry. It was the wrong thing to do."

"It was worse than wrong. It was unprofessional and dishonest."

"Stay cool," Dema told himself. "Let him say what he wants."

"Jim, I'll be honest. I don't know what I'm going to do about this. But one thing I can promise. If I ever catch you holding out on me again, I'll have your head on a silver platter. . . . Do you understand?"

"Yes, sir."

"Now get out of here."

"Do—"

"I said get out."

Dema rose; the detective stayed seated. "Are you coming?" the younger man asked.

"No! I'm going to have a very stiff drink—alone."

Dema left. For a minute or two, Marritt just sat there rubbing his forehead. . . . "Do I want a drink?"

he wondered. "Forget it. All I want is to go home. . . . Why do things like this always have to happen? . . . 'Professional conflict.' Christ! . . . I should have asked how long he'd known Doug Nicholas was a dealer. . . . Christ, again! The address book! Dema's name must have been on the missing page. I'll bet he's the one who took it. . . . Oh, fuck! It all fits together. Dema killed Doug Nicholas. . . . But how do I prove it?"

CHAPTER 25

Aggy sat in her apartment and stared at the wall. The pattern of leaves was frightening. She couldn't remember how she had gotten home from Dr. Hoffmann's office. The token was still in her pocket so it hadn't been by subway. The money was all in her wallet so it wasn't by cab. She must have walked. That was it. She had walked.

Eight-thirty P.M. The phone rang, but she refused to answer it. She lay face down on her bed, still clothed, with her arms crossed beneath her chest, one foot resting on the arch of the other. It was a position she had found after years of lying frightened on her back when the leaves cast shadows on the wall.

"Don't move," she told herself. "Lie still." But even as she lay motionless, her mind wandered toward dark corners, into a delirium much like the one endured when she suffered measles as a child. The bedroom walls had been papered with huge white magnolias on a background of blue. Day after day, Aggy lay on her bed, holding her favorite doll. Then one night, the doll slipped toward the edge of the sheet's turning. She tried to save it but was too slow in moving, and watched in horror as her only child slid into the dark crevasse between bed and wall. Tears of fear bathed her rash-marked face. Straining, exerting, she had managed to push the bed away from the wall and force herself into the space below but, when she did, the doll wasn't there.

Aggy recalled herself, the child. The memory wouldn't fade. She reminded herself that, when she was better, she had gotten up and looked in her toy chest and the doll was there. It was safe, just as her mother had assured—because her mother had picked the doll up and put it where it belonged.

Aggy rolled over and sat up. Since then, it had always been with a small twinge that she reached behind her bed if anything fell. So what now? She wanted to assure herself that the doll wasn't there. She sat for a while, telling herself it was stupid, but the urge remained, strong enough that finally she sensed there must be a reason why. She struggled, but her mind gave her nothing. Why was she thinking of it now? . . . "Do it."

She turned and pushed with both hands against the wall until the bed moved. And then she reached down where it was dark and groped for whatever was there. Her hair fell, covering her face, and she pushed it aside. "Find what's there! Find the doll!"

There were motes of dust. A cockroach fled the light, its hard red body scurrying along the hardwood floor. There were bobby pins, paper clips and a ball-point pen. Several pennies . . . And something more, leaning against the molding, completely in shadow, narrow and hard. *Aggy took it in her hands and raised it to the light—ugly; long; a bread knife, its blade and handle caked with blood.*

She didn't cry out or scream. She didn't move or even change her breathing. She was beyond all that now. She just sat while something passed across her face, and then tears were streaming like a river down her cheeks. She stayed that way for a long time, wondering why and how it had happened. Because in the end, Doug had gotten what he deserved, but she hadn't meant to kill him and, for the life of her, she couldn't remember doing it, not even now—but the knife was there.

And finally, she decided she needed someone. And in truth, there wasn't anyone to call except Rubes. Rubes, who was weak. Rubes, who so desperately wanted *her* to care. So she picked up the phone and, a few minutes later, Rubes was at her apartment. As always, Rubes was there.

"I found this," she said. And she held the knife out in her hand.

"Where?"

"I don't know."

"I asked you a question—where?"

"Behind the bed . . . next to the wall . . ."

He was more in control than she had expected—almost like Matt. "Let me have it," he said.

"Why?"

"You're in no shape to hold onto it. I'll turn it in to the police tomorrow."

She gave him the knife. And then something he did—or rather, didn't do—surprised her. He didn't offer to stay. Maybe he was angry because she hadn't treated him very well lately. Maybe he was scared. Rubes took the knife and left. And then again, she was alone, feeling as though everything that had come into her life before was a momentary dream and that reality was here. But what was happening? How had she gotten to where she was?

The clock read three-ten. Morning or afternoon? It was dark. . . . Three-ten in the morning. Aggy's eyes focused on the wall. She could see right through it, through the plaster, through the electrical wiring out into the hall.

He stood in the doorway across the hall, knocked sharply, and Doug let him in.

"What are you doing here, Reuben? You know

better than to come here at three o'clock in the morning. You'll wake the whole building."

Reuben . . . *REUBEN!*

That was the poison she'd been carrying in her system. For six weeks, she had known. She had known the night it happened. *Rubes had done it.*

CHAPTER 26

Aggy sat motionless in the corner, her back thrust protectively against the wall. Four o'clock . . . five A.M. . . . Thin shafts of light crept over the windowsill and across the studio floor.

She remembered now . . . six weeks ago. Rubes at the door . . . voices . . . the sounds of battle escalating into war. Then all had been quiet, an inner force propelling her from the safety of bed out into the corridor. The door to Doug's apartment was ajar. She looked inside. Rubes was gone. Doug lay on the floor in the center of the room. Part of his face was missing and his tongue was hanging down his throat, which had been cut open. Cranberry poured from his veins.

What she had done, where she had gone, she didn't remember. She had picked up the knife—that much she knew. After that, there was a dark, ever-deepening void.

Aggy looked at the clock. It was seven A.M. She needed help. It was cold. The Manhattan telephone directory lay on the floor. Clasping it with both hands, she frantically began turning pages . . . Reuben . . . Reuben . . . James . . . Lawrence . . . Matthew. Matthew P. Reuben . . . 310 East 69th Street . . . 871-6590. Matt was stronger than Rubes. Aggy picked up the phone and dialed. Four rings . . . Matt answered.

"It's Aggy. I have to talk with you. It's urgent."

Silence.

"Are you there? It's Aggy. Say something."

"I'm here," he answered.

"Matt, I need help. I'm scared."

"What's the matter?"

She pressed the receiver harder against her ear. "Can you come here . . . now . . . please." Her voice was desperate. "Matt, I'm in trouble."

"All right. I'll get dressed and come over."

"Hurry . . . please."

"Look," he commanded. "Get hold of yourself. Take a long bath or something. I'll be there as soon as possible."

Aggy put the receiver back on the phone and waited . . . Seven-twenty . . . seven-thirty . . . At ten to eight, the buzzer sounded. Trembling, she buzzed Matt in and rushed to meet him at the top of the stairs.

"Hello," he said.

Just hello. That was all. Hello and a gentle smile, as though by simply willing it he could make the world right again. Aggy looked up, and he put both arms firmly on her shoulders.

"Are you all right?"

"I guess so," she answered. "I had a bad night."

"What happened?"

"I know who killed Doug Nicholas."

He relaxed his grip and looked her over.

"I heard a name," she said. "Suppose I heard a name . . . I could believe it, couldn't I?"

"You're talking in riddles."

The words tumbled out, crammed between uneven breaths. "I heard Rubes's name. Right before Doug said it was three o'clock in the morning, I heard Rubes's name. And then I heard Rubes inside. I heard them arguing, I heard fighting, and afterward I saw Doug's body."

Matt looked hard into her eyes.

"I heard him."

"You've got to be wrong. Rubes isn't capable of something like that."

"Matt, I heard him."

"You're wrong."

"No, I'm not."

Matt stared. She was holding firm.

"There's something more . . . The knife."

"What knife?"

"I found it—the knife that killed Doug Nicholas. I found it the night of the killing and, last night, before I realized, I gave it to Rubes."

"Oh, Jesus!"

"Matt! What am I going to do?"

The world seemed to stop. Finally, Matt spoke again. "Have you told anyone?"

"No."

"He's my brother. You have to protect him."

Aggy shook her head. "I'm frightened. Help me."

Matt began to pace. "All right. You're wrong. You have to be, but I'll help. You're sure you haven't told anyone?"

"Positive."

"Don't."

"What can I do?"

"I don't know. I need time to think. I'll talk to you later today. Maybe tomorrow. In the meantime, call me at home if you need help." He looked at the bedraggled figure in front of him as though assessing her worthiness, then reached out and cradled her head between his hands. For a moment, she thought he might hold her in his arms, but the moment passed and he backed away. "Try not to worry," he said with calm reassurance. "Everything will be all right. I promise. Now lock the door and go to sleep. You'll never make it to work this morning."

Aggy smiled. "See, I'm not crazy after all. I heard it. I really did."

Sleep was elusive. Aggy lay in bed with her eyes open as the hands of the clock rotated by. Twelve noon . . . one in the afternoon . . . the morning . . . last night . . . everything was a blur. Matt would help. He'd promised. Thank God for Matt. Three weeks ago, she hadn't even known him; now her future was in his hands. Three weeks ago, she hadn't even known him . . .

Aggy sat up in bed and began to shake. A wave of fear more convulsive than any before was sweeping through her. It lodged in her stomach and paralyzed her chest and arms. She wanted to cry, but her throat was locked.

"What are you doing here, Reuben? You know better than to come here at three o'clock in the morning. You'll wake the whole building."

Rubes was the only Reuben she had known then. She had assumed it was him.

It could have been Matt.

Rubes had the knife . . . She'd just told Matt . . . "Oh, God! Someone, please help!"

CHAPTER 27

Aggy stumbled from bed and tore at the pages of the Manhattan telephone directory.

New York City Police Dept . . . 20th Precinct . . . 122 West 82nd Street . . . Marritt would be at the police station. If any sanctuary remained, it would be with him . . . Down the stairs . . . Through the vestibule.

The streets were growing dark as she stepped outside.

"Schwa, baby, schwa."

Aggy turned.

An old man—unshaven, a bum—staggered toward her, a pint bottle of whiskey in his hand. "Schwa, baby."

"Go away," she cried. "Leave me alone." But it really didn't matter that the bum was there, and she knew it, because everything was coming in waves, sweeping over her, and the undercurrent was sure to drag her down.

"Schwa, baby, schwa."

"Leave me alone."

She made her way past Broadway, then up Amsterdam, over to Columbus Avenue. Outside a squat gray concrete building, the curb was lined with blue and white cars.

"This must be it," she realized. "All these police cars. This must be where Marritt works."

The desk sergeant glanced up from the newspaper

in front of him as Aggy walked in. She looked like she'd been tripping—bloodshot eyes, disheveled hair, shirt hanging out of her jeans down below the back of her jacket.

"Excuse me," Aggy said softly. "Is Lieutenant Marritt in?"

"Sorry."

She hesitated, flustered. "I mean . . . do you know when he'll be here?"

"Afraid not. Today and tomorrow are his days off. My best guess would be Sunday."

"Oh."

She didn't move. The sergeant wanted to finish reading his newspaper. "He's not here, honey. Go home and sleep it off."

"Sleep what off?"

"Come on, kid. Your eyes are wide as buttons, and you talk like you got peanut butter in your mouth. Who are you trying to fool? Go home before I have to book you."

He said it almost kindly, as though he was doing her a favor.

"But I want to see Lieutenant Marritt. It's about—"

"I'll take it."

Aggy turned and stared up at Dema.

"It's no problem, Sergeant. Lieutenant Marritt and I are familiar with this woman and her problem. Let me take her upstairs to the office."

Aggy shrank back against the wall. "No!"

The sergeant was losing patience. "Look, lady! Don't be a psycho. Just do what the patrolman tells you."

Firmly, Dema took her by the arm and led her upstairs. "You're lucky I was on duty tonight," he said for the benefit of anyone who might be listening. "Usually, I don't work this late."

At the door to the office, she balked. "I want to see Lieutenant Marritt."

"I think it would be better if you said whatever you have to say to me. Then, if need be, I'll call Marritt."

"I want to see Lieutenant Marritt," she repeated, clinging to the frame of the door.

Dema backed into the room and beckoned her in. "If you have something to say, say it to me."

She didn't move, clinging stubbornly to the frame. Dema crossed back to where she stood and began prying her hand away.

"You'd better let go," he warned, putting his mouth to her ear. And then he saw she was holding on as an involuntary reflex, and the pressure was turning her fingernails white. So with his free arm, he pulled the door shut, not hard but hard enough to tap against her fingers until she let go and he was able to draw her into the room beside him.

"Sit down," he ordered.

"Let me go. Let me go, or I'll tell everyone about you."

"It's too late, Miss Tilden; I've already told Marritt everything you know. There's nothing you can do now to hurt me."

She stood mute, terror in her eyes. And then suddenly, Dema realized he had played it all wrong. It had been a mistake to respond with Marritt to the first radio call. He shouldn't have asked to be on the assignment. And above all, he should never have gone to Agatha Tilden's apartment alone.

"Go home," he told her.

Aggy looked around.

"Go home," he repeated. "There's nothing more for either of us to do."

Confused, not fully believing, she backed out of

the room. . . . Down the stairs, out onto the street. . . . Go home. . . . It was dark and the night was cold. Alone, whimpering, she staggered on . . . 82nd Street . . . Broadway . . . West End Avenue . . . She kept walking. . . . On the steps to her apartment, two figures were waiting. She turned, but it was too late. They had already seen her. Trembling, she came closer until she saw their faces. They were strangers. She didn't recognize either one.

"Hey, lady. Does Doug Nicholas live here?"

"No."

"He used to, but his name ain't on the mailbox anymore."

"He doesn't live here."

"Are you sure?"

"He doesn't live here. Go away."

Aggy turned her key in the lock and, as the door opened, saw the shadow of a figure looming behind her.

"It's only me," Rubes said. "Nice people you have sitting on your doorstep."

She fell back against the wall. "What are you doing here?"

"I came over to say hello."

"You usually call first."

"I didn't realize it was a formal requirement." He looked her over from top to bottom. "You look awful. Are you all right?"

"I had a bad night," she answered. "I'm going to sleep now."

Rubes smiled. "In the vestibule? Come on, I'll walk you upstairs."

There was no strength left to resist. Aggy led and Rubes followed. Upstairs, she fumbled with her keys, then inserted the larger of the two in the upper lock on her door.

"You've got the wrong key," Rubes said impatiently. "The safety lock uses the small one."

Inside, he closed the door behind them.

"Anything new?" he asked, taking a seat on the sofa.

She didn't answer.

"Matt tells me you're seeing a psychiatrist. Is that right?"

She had to say something. "I saw him, but I don't think it will help."

"I suppose that's right. I don't believe in psychiatry."

Why didn't he go home? Please go home.

"Do you think the cops know you've been holding out on them?"

"I don't want to talk about it."

Rubes smiled nervously. "Okay, but you seem awfully frightened."

"I'm fine."

"You don't look it."

"I can take care of myself."

Again silence. Rubes stepped forward. "Stay away," Aggy thought. "Please stay away."

He was coming closer.

"Get out," she pleaded.

"What's wrong with you?"

Still no answer.

Rubes's mind was spinning. "What's wrong?"

"Nothing."

"You're losing control."

"Stay away. I'm afraid of you."

He was even closer.

"Aggy, what's—" And then his voice went hollow. "You . . . you . . . think—"

He was almost on top of her. Desperately, she grabbed a bottle of wine off the dining table and pointed it in his direction.

"Get out!"

He reached forward. Savagely, she smashed the bottle against the wall and brandished the jagged edges.

"Get out," she shrieked. "Get out or I'll kill you."

"What—"

"Get out."

Rubes shrank back, frightened. "Get hold of yourself. What are you doing?"

Again there was silence. Slowly, Aggy let the broken bottle drop to her side. "I'm sorry," she said at last. "I just want to be left alone. Please go."

"I don't understand you."

"You don't have to. I just want you to go."

For a moment, they stood facing each other, immobile. Then Rubes spoke, softly. "All right. But before I go, I want to ask you one question. I've been wondering all week—did you get the flowers?"

"What flowers?" she started to ask. And then she realized what he was talking about, and she started to laugh, a fragile up-and-down hysterical laugh. Because here she was, scared senseless about going insane and maybe being hacked to pieces by a crazed murderer, and sad pathetic Rubes was worrying about love notes and roses.

"Yes," she said. "I got the flowers."

"What did I do wrong?"

"Do we have to, now?"

"It's important. What did I do wrong?"

"Nothing! You didn't do anything wrong. It's who and what you are." And then a wave of compassion swept over her, and she had to say one thing more. *"Rubes, don't you understand? You've been imagining things between us that never were."*

In that moment, it was as though his life had left him.

"All right," he said, backing toward the door. "If you want me, I'll be at home."

He left. Aggy double-locked the door. "Take a deep breath," she told herself. "Get control." . . . Maybe something to drink would help. She went to the refrigerator, pulled out a carton of orange juice, and poured it too fast into a glass on the counter so it spilled. She took a sponge to wipe it up. Instinctively, she knew something was wrong. And then she realized that the hook on the kitchen bulletin board next to "Tilden's Laws of Nature" was empty. The extra keys to her apartment were missing.

CHAPTER 28

Aggy sat motionless on the floor, huddled in a corner away from the door. A solitary light burned from the ceiling above. Her hands rested gently on her lap, covered by a gray wool blanket.

He'd be coming soon, whoever *he* was. Probably Rubes; he'd been there just a few hours before. But Matt could have taken the keys that morning; or even Dema, when he'd been in the apartment four days ago. Someone had them.

"I'm not crazy," she said out loud. "I'm not." Her eyes never left the door. "Why does everyone have to die alone?"

BZST!

The intercom.

"Go away."

BZST . . .

It smashed at her ears.

BZST . . . BZZZZST . . .

"Stop it! Whoever you are! What do you want?"

"Delivery for Agatha Tilden."

Oh, shit! Rubes again—more flowers.

BZZZZST . . .

"All right! Stop! I'll take the goddamn flowers."

She buzzed the delivery man in . . . and waited . . . A knock on the door . . . Aggy opened it a fraction of an inch.

"*NO!*" she shrieked.

Dema shoved hard and barreled in.

"NO! SOMEONE, HELP!"

Blindly, she dove for the door, but he blocked her charge and grabbed at her hair.

"HELP! PL—"

His entire hand clamped over her face. She couldn't breathe. Desperately, she struggled to break free, but it was no use. He was too strong and there wasn't any air. He was going to beat her to death; everything was growing blurred. He was talking, but she couldn't hear. Her lip was bleeding. She kicked and clawed but Dema held firm, and she was dizzy because the oxygen supply had been cut off from God knows where, and . . .

"Stop screaming! Just for a minute, please!"

Aggy fell limp and Dema drew back his hand, letting her slide to the floor.

"Are you all right?"

"Go away."

"Don't scream. The last thing I want is to hurt you. Just stay where you are and listen."

Her lip was still bleeding.

"I'm sorry. That's all I came here to say. Everything I did with you from the start was wrong."

She couldn't remember tasting her own blood before. What was he saying?

"Tonight, at the station house, I saw how frightened you were. I had no business threatening you. I'm not like that. I want to explain."

"Go away."

"I will; I promise. But first, let me tell you what happened and why. Doug Nicholas and I were lovers. You know that. He was a dealer. You know that too." Slowly, Dema knelt down until his eyes were level with hers. "And you and I both thought he was a friend. We were wrong. He treated me like he treated you and, at the end, I had less use for him than you did; but I didn't kill him."

"How do I know that?"

"Because I think you know who did. Doug bragged about sleeping with you, like he bragged about all his women. And when you turned up pregnant, he bragged about that too. I have to know—did you kill Doug Nicholas?"

"I want you to go," Aggy said softly. "I want you to leave me alone."

"You haven't answered my question."

"And I don't intend to." Her strength was starting to return. "Look, Dema-or-whatever-your-name-is. I've had as much of you as I can take. You've threatened my life. You've broken into my home. You're a stinking faggot, and it turns my stomach to look at you. I want you out, now."

His voice showed just a trace of anger. "All right," he said. "I'll leave you alone. But I want some answers, and I intend to get them."

Eleven o'clock . . . midnight . . . The clock ticked relentlessly on. Somewhere in Aggy's mind, the thought lodged that her keys were still missing. . . . Maybe they were under the bed. Wasn't that where she'd found the knife? "What are you doing here at three o'clock in the morning, Reuben? You'll wake the whole building." What if it was all in her mind? If Dema had the keys, he wouldn't have needed the delivery-man ploy to get in. That left Matt, and Rubes. What if they came *together?* . . .

One A.M. . . . the anniversary hour of Doug Nicholas's death was fast approaching. "He *will* come," Aggy told herself. "He will. I have to be ready for him." She looked around. "I wish I had a cannon. I'd aim it at the door and—" The cupboard! She rushed toward it. Dishes and pans; she pushed them aside. Two cups dropped and shattered on the floor. From the top shelf, an old aluminum pot beckoned. Aggy grabbed it and put it on top of the stove.

"What else? Oil! . . . Corn oil!" . . . Back to the cupboard . . . She reached for a jar . . . Thirty-two ounces . . . Almost full . . . Golden yellow; not much of a smell. She poured the oil into the pot and turned the burner on.

On the stairs, footsteps sounded.

"Not yet," she pleaded. "Not before it's ready."

Second floor . . . third . . . The intruder drew closer.

"The sword! I can use the sword."

Tarnished, curved, her Confederate cavalry cutlass hung on the wall. Seizing the hilt, Aggy tore the weapon from its mooring and moved to the door. Just across the threshold, the intruder halted.

"Now," she told herself, holding the sword in one hand, grasping the door with the other. "Now, before he's ready."

She flung the door open. "If you move," she warned, "I'll kill you."

Rubes dropped his hands to his side.

Aggy stepped back, brandishing the cutlass on high. "Come in," she ordered. "Isn't that what you wanted? Come in and close the door behind you."

"You're—"

"Shut up," she growled. "Shut up or I'll carve you into a stinking bloody mess."

Her eyes on his, she backed into the center of the room. Rubes followed, closing the door behind him.

"Raise your hands," she ordered, retreating to the corner.

He did.

"Now sit."

Rubes lowered himself onto the floor. "Can I explain?"

"There's nothing to explain. You came to kill me."

Rubes measured the distance between them. She was beyond reach.

"I didn't come here to kill you," he said with uncharacteristic calm. "I came to see if you were all right."

"At three o'clock in the morning?"

"Yes."

"Did you ever hear of the telephone?"

"I wasn't home. I was out on the street. The downstairs door was unlocked, so I came up."

"It's past your bedtime—a little late to go walking."

"I had a lot on my mind."

"I'll bet you did."

"Look," he said, rising to one knee, contemplating a lunge. "You're upset and I know it, but—"

"Get down," she snapped. "Sit!"

He sank back on the floor.

"You killed him," she said. "You killed Doug Nicholas and now—"

Again, footsteps echoed. Very slowly and deliberately . . . second floor . . . third . . . Aggy motioned Rubes toward the door. "Open it," she hissed.

Rubes did. "You'd better come in," he mumbled to the startled figure in front of him.

"Well, well," Aggy mocked. "Brother Matt." Hands shaking, she pointed the sword in his direction. "Do come in."

Startled, Matt stepped into the room.

"Which one of you has the keys," she demanded.

"Not me," Matt said. "I'm the one you called for help, remember?"

"Not at three o'clock in the morning."

Matt shrugged. "When I came in, the downstairs door was open." His eyes turned toward the sword. "Put it down."

"No."

He took a step forward.

"Stay where you are," she warned.

The oil! Frantically, she retreated toward the kitchen alcove. Matt advanced, one step at a time. Aggy let the sword drop and reached for the oil. The bottom half of the pot was scorched brown. Inside, tiny bubbles sizzled and swirled.

"That's far enough. One step more, and this oil goes all over your pretty-boy face."

Matt stopped . . . and waited.

Her legs ached. She wanted to sit, or at the very least lean against the wall for support. Rubes stood near the door. Matt dropped back a step to be closer to his brother.

"They're conspiring," she thought. "They're in this together."

"Why did you do it?" she asked aloud. "Why did you kill Doug Nicholas?"

Neither brother answered.

"Was it the money?"

Still no response.

"You came tonight for me, didn't you? That's why you took the keys from the bulletin board. So you could get in and destroy me."

"If you're so sure one of us killed him," Matt challenged, "call the police."

"I tried. They won't help."

"That's not the real reason," he pressed. "You

won't call the police because you know this is all in your mind. Neither of us had any reason to kill Doug Nicholas."

"You had the same reason everyone else had—two hundred thousand dollars."

"That doesn't mean anything. If Doug Nicholas was killed for his money, you could have done it. You're a lot more likely to have known where it was hidden than we are."

She was getting dizzy. She hadn't slept in forty-eight hours. She wouldn't be able to hold on much longer. The brothers were blurring. Now Rubes was talking.

"If I stole your keys, I'd have them in my pocket. I don't. You can look for yourself."

"If that's a trick to bring me closer, it won't work."

"There's no trick."

"Prove it."

Very slowly, his eyes never leaving hers, Rubes took his jacket off and slid it across the floor. Kneeling by the garment, Aggy fished through the pockets until she was satisfied they were empty.

"Now your pants."

"What!"

"Your pants."

Rubes unbuckled his belt and dropped his trousers, then shoved them forward. Again, Aggy checked the pockets . . . a wallet . . . comb . . . Rubes's mailbox key and the key to his apartment . . . a soiled handkerchief. Kicking the jeans aside, she focused her attention on Matt. "You next. Take off your jacket and pants."

"Look," Matt protested. "This is silly."

"I thought you loved to drop your pants in front

of women. . . . Never mind. You disgust me." She turned toward Rubes. "Search him."

Rubes reached for Matt's jacket.

"Don't!"

A knife with a five-inch blade clattered to the floor.

Long silence.

"I carry it at night for protection," Matt said.

Rubes stared down at the knife.

"What else is in the jacket?" Aggy demanded.

Rubes didn't move.

"The keys," she cried. "Find the keys."

Rubes reached into Matt's pocket. There—a pair of keys attached to the chain that had once hung on the kitchen bulletin board.

"Drop them," Aggy ordered.

Rubes did as told.

"Now move away from him."

Rubes took two steps to the side.

Aggy stared at Matt. A thin wisp of steam rose from the pot of oil. "I'm going to empty this onto your pretty-boy face. Ten seconds from now, your own brother won't be able to stand the sight of you."

"You're a lunatic."

"That's right. You made me this way. And you can't reason with a lunatic, so don't even try."

"I didn't mean to kill him. Let me explain."

"There's nothing you can say."

"Then you can destroy me when I'm done." Matt had to keep talking, keep her at bay until an opening presented itself. "Let me explain; please! I didn't mean to kill him. I only went to buy—honest! Rubes gave me Doug's name right after you told him Doug was a dealer. I bought from him once or twice, then went back to buy again. I didn't mean to do anything wrong. Then I got to his apartment, I looked at him, and saw him for what he was."

"You're wasting your breath."

"I was all hyped up, I get that way sometimes. Doug was prancing around the apartment, bitching, saying things like it was three o'clock and I'd wake the whole building. And it was like he was coming on to me. There was a knife lying on the table next to an apple. I grabbed it to keep him away and then I realized that, if I robbed him, he couldn't report it to the police. All his money came from drugs. There was nothing he could do or say. So I grabbed the knife and asked where the money was. It was almost a joke but, before I knew what was happening, it was real. Then everything came all at once. He wouldn't tell me, so I held the knife to his throat. He still wouldn't break so I slashed his Adam's apple, almost without trying. He began to bleed but he still wouldn't talk, so I stuck the knife in his side. Then he pointed to the ceiling panel. The money was there, but it was too much. I was afraid he'd retaliate after I'd gone and, Rubes, he was queer. It was like the whole thing was sexual. Everything just got out of hand. He started to scream and I shoved the knife in his back. I didn't want the neighbors to hear him and call the police, so I had to shut him up. I shoved the knife in again, but he kept screaming, and I kept pushing it in until the screaming stopped. But, Rubes, it was justified. Don't you see? Doug Nicholas was a dealer; someone who ruined lives. He was a bum, and he would have wound up like one of those toothless old men you see on the sidewalk begging for a handout on cold winter days."

Rubes, in a trancelike daze, stared at his brother.

"The cops were right. There was over two hundred thousand dollars in the apartment. Enough for me; enough for all three of us."

Now was the time. Very slowly, hands raised in an I'm-not-armed position, Matt moved forward.

"Get back," Aggy warned. "I have the pot."

"I know, but I think it's cooled off by now. There's no harm in a pot of lukewarm vegetable oil."

Aggy froze.

"Besides, you have no intention of throwing that oil. We both know that."

He was almost on top of her.

Aggy fell back . . . "Help." It was a whisper.

Bending low, Rubes picked the knife off the floor.

"Please help."

Matt's hands reached for her throat.

Stumbling, Rubes reached forward and pushed the tip of the blade against the space between his brother's shoulders. Matt stiffened, his hands still in the air.

"I told you, I didn't mean to kill Doug Nicholas. I only wanted to buy."

"And tonight?"

Matt flinched, the evidence of intent planted squarely against the center of his back. Five seconds . . . Ten . . . "I'm your brother," Matt said at last. "Without me, there's no one."

"You've drawn from that well too often."

"Maybe so, but it's still not dry. And besides, I don't think you could kill anyone, especially not your own brother."

Silence. Aggy looked on, trembling.

"We'll make a deal," Matt said. Hands still in the air, he took a step forward and the pressure of the knife eased. "I'm not going to hurt anyone. I'm going to keep my hands high and walk out of this apartment. I want a two-hour head start to pick up the money and, after that, I'll be gone. I don't care what you do. You can call the police or go home and forget this ever happened. Either way, as far as I'm concerned, it doesn't matter. I won't be back. Neither of you will ever see me again."

There was no answer.

"I'm going now," Matt said, taking a first tentative step toward the door.

The knife was still pointed in his direction.

"Don't worry, I'm going."

"Two hours," Rubes told him. "That's all."

THOMAS HAUSER is a New York City author and attorney. His first book, *Missing,* was nominated for a Pulitzer Prize and adapted into the much-celebrated Costa-Gavras film starring Jack Lemmon and Sissy Spacek. He is also the author of *The Trial of Patrolman Thomas Shea* and *Ashworth & Palmer,* released to wide critical acclaim.

Mr. Hauser writes a monthly legal column for *McCall's,* and has written for the *New York Times, New York* magazine and numerous other publications. He is currently at work on his latest novel and lives in Manhattan.

"DEEPLY DISTURBING...READS LIKE THE SCENARIO OF A HITCHCOCK THRILLER."
LOS ANGELES TIMES

missing.

BY THOMAS HAUSER

A young American in Chile accidentally stumbles onto evidence of covert U.S. involvement in the overthrow of the Allende government—and is murdered afterwards. This is the chilling account of Charles Horman's last days—and of his family's determination to learn the truth about his death.

"DEVASTATING...A chilling reminder of how far our public servants may sometimes go in the pursuit of the national interest." The New York Times Book Review

"An excellent book." Village Voice

The film starring Jack Lemmon and Sissy Spacek, and directed by Costa-Gavras, won the GOLDEN PALM GRAND PRIX at the 1982 Cannes Film Festival.

Other Avon books by Thomas Hauser are AGATHA'S FRIENDS (82222-9/$2.50) and THE TRIAL OF PATROLMAN THOMAS SHEA (62778-7/$3.50).

An AVON Paperback 58834-X/$2.95